Kenyan Quest

by

Jack Rosshirt

Kenyan Quest

Copyright 2002
by
Jack Rosshirt
Cover design by Renny James

ISBN 0-9717868-1-X

WordWright.biz
P.O. Box 1785
Georgetown, Texas 78627

Printed in the United States of America

This book is dedicated to my wife, Alana
and my sons and their families.
John and Sharon, John Leo, John Marshall,
Will and Ryan;
Tom and Molly, Nicholas and Benjamin;
David,
Dan and Jean, Danny and Kathryn Alana;
and especially to
Matt
November 9, 1962 – June 15, 1986
the best writer of us all.

Table of Contents

Chapter 1.............*Return to Marsabit*...........................1

Chapter 2 ....*Houston* 11

Chapter 3.............*The Houston Meeting* 23

Chapter 4.............*Vienna* 30

Chapter 5.............*Northern Ireland* 49

Chapter 6.............*Arrival in Nairobi* 64

Chapter 7.............*The Embassy Visit*......................... 72

Chapter 8.............*The Norfolk Hotel Reception* 81

Chapter 9.............*Visit to the Minister* 92

Chapter 10 ....*Chalbi Desert Drive*.....................104

Chapter 11 ....*North Horr* 123

Chapter 12 ....*The Discovery* 132

Chapter 13 ....*Sebastian's Story*..........................143

Chapter 14 ....*Monsignor Juraj*..........................169

Chapter 15 ....*The Decision* 184

Epilogue..197

About the Author 200

Acknowledgments

I wish to thank all those who helped bring this book to fruition, whether by reading drafts and commenting or by encouraging me to proceed. Just because I ignored your suggestions doesn't mean I didn't appreciate them.

Thanks, also, to the members of the Novel in Progress group of the Writers' League of Texas who read and commented on portion of this book.

Special gratitude goes to Mindy Reed of the Author's Assistant of Austin, Texas and Joan R. Neubauer of Word Wright International, Georgetown, Texas for their support and encouragement.

Author's Note

Many of the events used as background in this story actually occurred, and the descriptions of the places are generally accurate. However, this is a work of fiction and not a precise history or description of events and people. Individual persons and actions are the invention of the author.

Chapter 1

Return to Marsabit

The German anthropologists stopped their Land Rover near a large outcrop in the otherwise flat desert. Even though it was hotter outside the air-conditioned vehicle they chose to sit in the shade of the rock, breathe the fresh air, eat a snack and drink some bottled water.

A few hundred meters away two Rendille natives rode their camels toward them. The Germans, having come to the Chalbi desert to study the nomad's life, welcomed the opportunity to meet with natives without having to track them across the wide wasteland.

The camels stopped fifteen meters from the men and made their unique herky-jerky descent into a sitting position. The riders slid to the ground and walked forward.

"Jambo, habari gani? How are you?" one of the Germans greeted the men in Swahili.

The visitors showed no sign of response as they circled the two men and the vehicle. The Germans thought their behavior strange, but as the Rendille were known as peaceful people the Germans only watched quizzically. When the nomads had half circled the men they reached under their flowing robes and each extracted an AK-47. Being careful not to hit the Land Rover, they gunned down the scientists with short bursts of fire, dropping the victims where they stood.

The natives turned the bloody bodies on their backs to make sure they were dead. They were. Quick brown hands emptied the pockets of the victims. The robed men took billfolds, watches, rings, boots and anything else that might be of value, including passports from the pouches hanging around the men's necks.

Without conversation, the robed figures moved the camels to the Land Rover, unloaded their possessions into it and released the camels. For the first time one of them spoke.

In Somali he said to his companion, "This should get us about $50,000 from one of the warlords in Mogadishu."

They climbed into the vehicle, checked the gas gauge and started driving northeast back to the civil war in Somalia.

છ છ છ

District Commissioner Joseph Kamala stood in the car park of his District headquarters in Marsabit looking down at what remained of two bloody carcasses. His men had found them in the desert under an umbrella of circling vultures. The patrol had arrived before the bones had been stripped clean but not before the eyes had been picked out and the stomachs ripped open. Kamala wished that the scavengers had finished their work erasing the evidence of the use of automatic weapons. From the remains, Kamala concluded the victims were the Germans who had passed through Marsabit a few days ago. He'd warned them. The victims had obviously met not nomads, but the shiftas, bandits from Somalia or the Sudan who moved into Kenya to poach ivory or steal cattle or camels.

The district commissioner stood at a well built six-foot tall. In his early fifties, his dark skin was more ebony than brown. He dressed in the military style inherited from the British, along with a governing system in which the district commissioners had unlimited power. He functioned as a combination governor, police chief, and commanding officer. Fortunately for the commissioners the Kenyans were basically peaceful because limited manpower and equipment precluded heavy-duty peacekeeping.

Kamala went to his office to radio the incident to Nairobi and to ask if they wanted the bodies sent down or whether someone would come up to investigate. If it weren't for their condition they'd be sent to Nairobi so the German Embassy could handle the paperwork required to ship the bodies out. Kamala shook his head in frustration. This was the second recent killing incident.

A year ago, two Italians on their way to the Italian supported Catholic medical mission near North Horr, a desert village one hundred miles northwest into the desert from Marsabit, were found shot in the desert with no clue of their murderers. At least the victims were not Americans, Kamala thought with some relief. For some reason, American deaths got more attention from the press, to the detriment of the tourist trade. Kamala had the bodies hosed off and moved to the air-conditioned storage building. He expected a visitor later today and the bodies would be off putting to say the least.

ααα ααα ααα

Shortly after four in the afternoon, the soldier on duty at the desk reported a Land Rover with one passenger had pulled into the car park.

"Send him in," Kamala instructed.

Matt Stark knocked on the door and walked into the commissioner's office. Matt stood about five-feet eleven inches. His mostly black hair, while seriously thinning on the top, was longer in back than when he had been a corporate executive. He weighed a solid one hundred and eighty pounds. A creased forehead set off his tanned face and laugh lines framed his green gray eyes. In his khaki clothes he looked like one of the characters in a World War II desert movie. The men shook hands.

"Matt, good to see you again." Kamala waved Matt to the chair opposite his desk. Kamala's office was military neat, with the requisite picture of the Kenyan president hanging on the wall behind his desk. The opposite wall held the unique green, black, and red horizontal striped Kenya flag with the shield and crossed spears in the center of it.

"Like a cool drink?" Kamala asked.

"I could use a Tusker," Matt said naming his favorite local beer. "Thanks."

Kamala pushed the buzzer on his desk. When a voice answered he asked for ice water and the beer. "Matt, before we get caught up in recollections, let me get my official duty out of the way. I understand you want to go out to your old area. You're free to go but it's not as safe as it used to be. I suggest that you finish your business in the Chalbi as soon as possible."

"What's going on, Joe?"

"Trouble. We picked up the bodies of two Germans not far from where you are going. A year ago we had two other visitors killed. We can't police the whole area between here and North Horr. Too much room for the shiftas to operate. I can't give you much protection but I can give you an escort on the drive to North Horr this time."

A smartly dressed soldier entered the room with beer, glasses, a pitcher of water and a bowl of ice. He placed the tray on the desk, saluted, turned on his heels and left.

"Ice." Matt raised an eyebrow. "You're getting decadent."

"Civilization marches on, even in the desert. I wish that were the only bad habit we picked up from the West." Kamala placed ice in his glass with tongs and poured Matt's glass three quarters full. "Cheers," he said handing him the glass.

"Cheers." Matt took a long pull on his beer.

"Getting back to the situation here. One of the nuns from the medical mission, Sister Columba, came in yesterday from Nairobi. They get up here on their own then we usually have my men, depending on how busy we are, escort them out to the mission and do a surveillance of the surrounding area. You can make the safari in two cars."

"Is that really necessary?"

"I think so. Look here, Matt."

Kamala walked to the large map of Kenya and the surrounding countries hanging on the wall. "The border with Sudan and Somalia is immensely long and wide open. Worse, it's not like it was in the old days when the tribes and bandits had cattle raids like soccer games. Then they had only spears, pangas, or simple firearms. Now, armed with AK-47s and other rapid-fire weapons, they outgun us. We can't contain them if they come in large groups. In the old days the Northwest Frontier District (NFD) was closed to most people. We may have to do that again. In the meantime, better safe than sorry."

Matt put his empty glass on the tray. "Thanks, Commissioner, I appreciate your interest. We'll make a quick drive around the old drill site and see what's left of the water wells and the landing strip. If we can locate the water wells it'll save us a lot of time and thousands of dollars looking for water at the next drilling. We'll get to North Horr as soon as possible."

Kamala sat back down behind his desk. "Matt, those well locations are going to be weathered over. You won't find anything."

"We left metal well heads on them so the locals could draw water. Maybe some of them are still lying around to help us spot the locations." Matt poured the rest of the beer into his glass.

"Another one?" Kamala asked.

Matt shook his head. "No thanks." He figured he could have another at the lodge.

"Be realistic," Kamala continued. "The tribesmen

will have picked up and sold any metal left or made something of it."

"Probably right, but we're here and ready to go. By the way, how's the mission doing? Strange as it seems I never got to North Horr when I was here before."

"Why not?"

"I was an office dude. I'd just fly up for the day and fly straight back to Nairobi. I never did any sight seeing."

"The mission's okay," Kamala continued. "Still give basic primary medical care to the nomads. They do a lot less preaching than a few years ago. If they get a serious case they radio me and I call for the Flying Doctors from Nairobi. Why they want to spend their lives in the desert is beyond me. When I retire I am going back to my Shamba where it's cool and green."

The commissioner knew his complaint about the desert was a bit overdone. While most of his territory was desert, he spent ninety percent of his time in his headquarters in the cool heights of the National Reserve at Marsabit. The reserve, almost 800 square miles in area had at its center a forested mountain including a lake. A large population of elephants and Greater Kudus as well as giraffe, hyenas and twenty to thirty other types of animals roamed the area. A sizable bird concentration seasonally included species from all over the world. At one time the park was the home of Ahmed, the largest elephant in Kenya, living under special protection of the president. However, not even presidential protection could prevent Ahmed from getting murdered for his tusks. All in all, Kamala had a posh assignment.

"Matt, are you really serious about looking for oil

here again? After you left, the French and Shell Oil drilled more wells, spent tens of millions of shillings, francs, guilders and dollars and found nothing. Why come back?"

"Oil people are optimists. Oil can only be found by drilling for it. They want to drill again."

Kamala cleared some papers from his desk. "Our people never understood how you spent all that money with no return. You recall the newspaper articles in the 'Standard' and the 'Times.' We thought the whole thing was a fraud. We can understand if you build a plant like General Motors because you can see a building, but not drilling some holes in the ground."

"It's hard to understand the risk if you're not in the business. This time the risk isn't so great because we eliminated some prospects."

"Okay. It's your money. Good luck, but don't ignore my warnings. At the first sign of trouble, head for the mission or return here. Whoever killed the Germans took their vehicle. They could still be around."

"Don't worry. We'll go straight to the mission, spend a couple of days checking for the wells then head back. We won't stop on the way back if we don't need supplies." Matt started to get up.

"One second, Matt. I've forgotten my manners in my concern for your safety. How's your wife? Carol, wasn't that her name? She seemed to enjoy Kenya. And your children? I recall you spoke of two, but they didn't come to Kenya."

"Thanks for asking. Carol died of cancer a year ago. If she were alive I wouldn't be here."

"I'm sorry, Matt. I remember her as loving the beauty of Kenya."

"She was very happy here. About the kids, our daughter, Sheila is a lawyer in Seattle with two children and a husband, a schoolteacher. Frank our son, works for a major bank in New York City. He's still unmarried. They seem to be happy and busy. How's your family?"

"They're well. Karen's an assistant curator at the Nairobi museum. Both Matthew and Ceal finished university in England and are working in London. Jobs are more plentiful there. We miss them. We see them once or twice a year. They're healthy and happy and that's the best we can ask. Well, Kwaheri, Matt. You do remember your Swahili enough to know that means goodbye?"

Matt laughed. "Kwaheri, Commissioner. That's about all I remember except for the first two words I learned: pombe baridi, cold beer. I'll keep in touch on the radio. Moses Mrabi, our geologist, and I are at the Marsabit Lodge tonight. We'll leave at dawn to try to get in as much mileage as we can before the heat hits full blast. Thanks again for your help."

"No problem, besides I got a call from the minister of energy's office to give you every assistance. I think they meant me to keep an eye on you. You're not up to something are you?"

"No," Matt said looking surprised. "Isn't such special attention unusual?"

"A little but it's not the first time. Anyway, look up Sister Columba at the lodge and coordinate your leaving. The guards and my vehicle will meet you at dawn."

The two friends shook hands again. Matt drove the short distance to the lodge, thinking about how much he missed Carol. He pulled into the car park and went into the bar. He'd look up the nun later.

Chapter 2

Houston

Sixty days before his arrival in Marsabit, Matt was dozing in his den in Austin when the phone woke him. Three sets of tennis in the morning, Texas heat and a couple of glasses of wine at lunch left him ready for an afternoon nap. Especially since he usually got up between five and five thirty. The early rising came from a combination of advancing age, early bedtime and an empty house. At night it was the opposite, he seldom made it through the ten o'clock news and his nightcap. Matt's doctor called the limited nighttime sleep a normal part of depression that most people experienced after the death of a spouse.

"Matt Stark," he said into the receiver.

"Matt, this is Pete Quanda in Houston."

Matt sat up. "Hey, Pete. How are you? Haven't seen you since your retirement party three or four years ago."

"Four to be exact. I'm fine. So's Sara. We're sorry to hear about Carol. We couldn't make the funeral. We were in South America."

"Thanks for the donation to the Cancer Fund. You on vacation?"

"No. I've been doing freelance negotiation."

"Doesn't sound like retirement to me."

Pete chuckled. "Well, after I retired I got a bunch of calls. First I turned 'em down but then the money got bigger and the wanderlust came back so I've taken a few assignments. It can be fun if you don't do it all the time."

"True. To what do I owe the honor?"

"I got a call the other day to work on a deal in Africa, more precisely your old stomping grounds, Kenya. I'm not interested and you're better suited for it. I told them about you. They want to talk."

"Who are they?"

"An independent, Big Star Oil. Two guys named Billy Bob Kelly and Big Tex Cernak."

"You're not serious."

"Sure am. They made a fortune in West Texas, kept most of it and diversified. They're still active in oil but they're also into real estate, shopping centers, automobile dealerships and sports franchises, you get the idea."

"Why do they want to fool around overseas? They could lose a bundle."

"Pride, envy, greed. Who knows? They sit around at the Petroleum Club and listen to their old buddies BS about killings they've made outside the US. They want a piece of it. It chaps their butts that they aren't international. Of course, their buddies don't tell them when they lose their asses in an overseas deal."

The fuzziness was leaving Matt's head and he started to focus on what Pete was saying. "What kind of deal is it?"

"Dunno. Once I knew I wasn't going to work it I

didn't ask any more."

"I'm not excited about running around since Carol died."

"Understandable, but you can't just sit out there on your duff in Lakeway. You'll rust to death."

"You've got a way with words, Pete, but you have a point. I've lost interest in a lot of things I used to enjoy. Even tennis is getting boring."

"Yeah, playing with the same ten people within a ten mile area."

"About right."

"Come on. You used to like meeting new people and challenges."

"Okay, I'll call them and see what they have to say."

"Way ahead of you friend. Thought you might hesitate, so I made an appointment for you with them for lunch Monday at the Petroleum Club. They're hot to move on this. Come on down Sunday. Stay with us. We'll get some old oil patch friends in for dinner Sunday night and you can meet the oil guys Monday."

Matt didn't know whether to be angry or flattered. He decided to let it go. "It'll be nice to see you and Sara. Be at your place between four and five. How'd those guys learn of the deal?"

"Beats me, ask them. Oh, yeah, don't be fooled by their names or Big Tex's appearance. Billy Bob went to some prep school in Connecticut and has a geology degree from Dartmouth. I don't know where Big Tex got his formal schooling but he comes from Chicago. His family was big in Democratic politics. They landed in Midland about the same time and hooked up. Somehow they had plenty of money behind them. Bought up lots of leases and were picking up whole companies at one time. Like I said, they were smart enough to diversify before things got bad. So they're still big players."

"Sounds like a fun pair." Matt jotted down their names. "At least I'll get a free dinner from you and a free lunch from them. Do you still live in the same place?"

"Yup. Just come in on I-10 and turn off at the Bingle Voss exit."

"I remember. See you Sunday evening. Thanks for the call."

"No problem. Bye"

Matt hung up the phone. "Well, Carol, this could be interesting. Let's hope so. Pete's right, I just can't sit here eating, drinking and reading the rest of my life. Wish you were here to go with me."

Carol was always ready for a trip. She went with Matt on as many overseas trips as business and the company would allow. A pretty, intelligent woman with short, blond hair, her presence was always appreciated at the social events surrounding an overseas negotiation. Her quick wit kept conversations from getting bogged down in too much business talk. All in all she was a pleasant traveling companion. He missed her.

⋘　⋘　⋘

Matt stopped halfway on his drive to Houston at Columbus to stretch his legs to make sure he wasn't too early. He had a couple of Lone Star beers to pass the time. He arrived at Pete's about four in the afternoon and popped a breath mint into his mouth before getting out of the car.

The three other couples invited to the Quanda's had worked at one time or another with Matt and had known Carol. Two of the couples had shared the same overseas assignments, and it had become a bonding experience. After an exchange of regrets and condolences over Carol's death, the mood lifted.

Over drinks they reviewed where everyone had located, what they were doing, grandchildren and deaths. Most had wine. Matt had a Stoli on the rocks. Sara's tasty Iranian dinner of yogurt soup and chello kabob was especially welcomed by the couples who had lived in Iran. After dinner drinks and coffee, the talk turned to recollections of working and living in Third World countries. Time had dimmed the bad memories so most of the recollections were pleasant and some very funny, even discounting the embroidery. The party broke up by eleven.

"Thanks for getting the group together. I enjoyed it." Matt said as he poured himself a nightcap.

"We did too. I'll show you where the coffee is and how the maker works. I'm a late sleeper so I probably won't see you in the morning," Sara said.

"I've got a golf game at seven," Pete added. "Got to beat the heat, so I might miss you, too. Make yourself at home."

"Thanks again. I'll probably leave mid-morning to run some errands and drive through the old neighborhood."

"Fine," Pete said. "Call me after the lunch. I want to

know if those characters are as big as they sound. I left a copy of my last consulting agreement in your room so you can have an idea of current general terms. Just double the figures when you talk to Billy Bob and Big Tex." Pete smiled when he said the names.

"I'll let you know one way or the other. I'll drive straight back to Austin after the lunch. I'll call you from home."

"Fine. Sleep well."

"Matt's spirits seemed to have picked up," Pete commented to Sara as they got into bed.

"They should have. He had enough to drink. I don't remember him as a heavy drinker."

"He wasn't," Pete said as he set the alarm clock.

"Probably part of his reaction to Carol's death," Sara said from under the covers. "Let's hope this job helps him snap out of whatever he's in. Nite."

ෆ   ෆ   ෆ

About six thirty the next morning Matt shook his tingling head, showered, dressed and went into the kitchen. He took coffee and juice over to the breakfast table to review the consulting contract Pete had left for him. His head cleared as he read slowly, making notes of the payments called for and other key provisions. Then he poured more coffee and settled in the den with the "Houston Chronicle" and "The New York Times." He sped through the Chronicle, except for the sports section, skipping over news of local crimes and other problems. He spent longer going through the Times. The overseas news had more interest for him. Especially stories about the places he'd lived or visited.

Unexpectedly, Sara came into the room, a cup of coffee in her hand.

"I thought you were a late sleeper," Matt said.

"Normally I am, but Pete woke me when he got up. I couldn't get back to sleep. I kept thinking of Carol and you. Wanted to see how you were doing."

"Sara, we're good friends, but please don't mother me."

"I'm just concerned Matt, don't be offended." She took a seat opposite Matt.

"Sorry." Matt sipped his coffee and looked off into space. After a short pause he said, "I really haven't talked about it much, but sometimes I'm sitting on the sofa at home watching television and turn to make some comment to her about what's on the tube, but she's not there. That's one reason I've come to Houston."

"It must be lonely."

"More than you can imagine. We had a good life: the kids, golf, tennis, charity work. I volunteered at a hospital. Carol was a child advocate in the court system. We planned to travel around the States."

"Sounds pleasant."

"It was while it lasted. It didn't last long enough."

"I've had friends die of cancer. How was it discovered?"

"It started from nothing. Carol went to her dermatologist to remove sunspots from her hands and face. Nothing she hadn't done before. While she was there the doctor noticed a raised portion under the skin on

17

her leg. Pretty atypical.

"Didn't bother her except she'd rubbed it from time to time. He asked her if she wanted him to take it out while she was there. She said, 'Sure, why not.' He excised it and sent it to the lab with the other cuttings. When she came back the next week for the lab results he told her it was melanoma. She didn't know what that was exactly but from his long face and demeanor she knew it was serious. He made appointments with a surgeon and an oncologist in Austin for her that same week. Then she knew it was serious. And we had thought it was just another skin deal you cut off and forgot about."

"It must have been shattering."

"Yeah, especially when the doctor told us about melanoma. It's a quick killer when it gets into the blood and lymph system."

"What happened next?" Sara put down her coffee to concentrate.

"A cat scan and an MRI. They found the primary site in the intestines. We visited an oncologist in Austin. He suggested that we not cut further in case we wanted to do vaccine protocol. They'd need her melanoma cells for the vaccine." Matt continued in a monotone as the pain of Carol's illness returned. "We went to another oncologist in Austin. He confirmed the diagnosis and suggested investigating protocols at some of the top cancer hospitals in the United States like M.D. Anderson in Houston, Sloan-Kettering in New York or the John Wayne Cancer Institute in Santa Monica."

"How'd you decide what to do?"

"After a lot of soul searching, research and

conversations with friends with cancer in Austin we decided to go M.D. Anderson in Houston." Matt continued. "We met with an expert in the skin cancer section, Dr. Nota Ramos. Over a four day period we had another complete workup, including removing lymph nodes."

"How did Carol hold up?"

"Better than I did."

Matt stood and started to pace. "M.D. Anderson's staff was supportive, but the emotional impact of all the patients moving around with various stages of cancer is shattering. Cancer is just a word to most people, but at M.D. Anderson it's people. Hundreds of people and their families from all over the world. All ages too. We didn't see the tiny ones but one of my worst memories was of a big handsome boy, obviously an athlete, with nothing below the knee on one leg." A quiver entered his voice.

Sara reached toward Matt. "Sorry, I didn't mean to upset you."

Matt grimaced in an attempt to smile. "No, No, it's all right. I'm sorry. I'm rambling. I haven't talked about it for sometime. I get a sick feeling in my stomach when I do, but after I'm finished I feel more peaceful."

"Keep talking if it helps. I'm not going anywhere."

"Thanks, Sara. Well, we ended up reading more about cancer than we ever knew existed. Stuff from organizations like the National Cancer Institute to more marginal material from all sorts of people. Some of it pretty weird. Spontaneous healing books are big, too."

"What was Carol's reaction?"

"She was pretty steady. After the exams, tests and

operation we met again with Dr. Ramos. He was very direct. The cancer was in a number of organs. It was at stage III. His opinion was that without treatment Carol would die in a matter of months, a year at the outside. We could do nothing or she could take chemotherapy and biological regimens, including interferon. He explained that these clinical trials had low success ratios. Carol would suffer chills, fevers, nausea, vomiting, diarrhea, rashes, hair loss, all the things you read and hear about. She'd spend considerable time in the hospital. One protocol required intensive treatment for a week or so then home until she got stronger, then back in for more treatment, then back home and repeating the cycle five or six times with no assurances of a cure. It's just a damn experiment. We got lots of advice but the final decision was ours."

Sara's voice grew soft. "How did you decide?"

"We focused in on what kind of life would Carol have. Was it a life at all? Ramos told us to go home think, pray and decide what we wanted to do. He reminded us that one of the effects of cancer is that the patient and their family become frightened, angry or depressed. We should expect it and take our time. He told us to call him anytime we wanted to talk."

"He sounds kind."

"He was. We were also lucky that we had good friends and good relationships with our kids. Carol had friends who had been through the difficulty of breast cancer treatment. Talking to all of them was helpful. We went to a support group but didn't find that helpful. We only went once or twice. Our situation just seemed different."

"What moved you one way or another?"

"That was really strange. We hadn't been regular church goers for quite a while. One evening we went downtown for an early dinner. We walked by a church. The door was open. For some reason we went in and sat down. I don't even recall the denomination. Outside the streets were empty. It was quiet. We sat there for some time. We didn't say anything. We both knew what we were thinking about. Finally, Carol said, 'Let's go.' As we did, a man came to close the door. He said he was surprised it was open because they kept it locked most of the time to keep out the street people."

"Strange."

"We drove home, opened some wine, a dry chenin blanc. Got some cheese from the fridge, a Havarti and a Vermont cheddar. We sat down in the den. Funny how you remember details.

"Carol looked at me and said, 'Matt, Ramos says the protocols will be high stress. I'll be horribly sick for most of the time. My chance of recovery is very low. I'm sixty years old. Our kids are grown and I've seen our grandkids come into the world. I can live decently without treatment for a month or a year. I think that I want to live as best I can for the days left to us. That means no treatment. If I were thirty or forty and had young kids I might feel differently. What do you think?'"

"What a difficult question," Sara said.

"Yes and no. Carol and I had been on the same wavelengths for most things over the years. Almost like mind reading. This was no different. I told her that I'd support whatever she wanted to do. We could travel, visit the kids and do what we could as things moved along. We had been holding hands. 'We've done some great things,' I said to her, 'Let's make this the best.' We sat there staring out the window into the darkness until we both fell asleep. Finally, Carol woke up and said, 'Matt, let's go to bed.'"

"We talked about the decision again the next morning, agreed to no treatment, and never looked back."

"You had a very good, a strong marriage."

"We did. That's what long years of marriage is supposed to do. Anyway, we managed to live a normal life for a few months. Got in one trip to Australia and a few shorter trips before she got too weak to travel. We transferred back to our doctor in Austin. He monitored the course of the cancer. As she got worse he gave her medication to ease her pain. Carol spent her last days at the Austin Hospice with people who were dedicated to easing her pain. We never regretted our decision. We enjoyed what we could and lived with the rest."

"Sorry Matt, it makes me weepy. If there's anything I can do let me know."

"You've already done a lot by setting up this meeting for me. If the project goes through, it should help me."

"I hope so." Sara gave Matt a hug. "Call us after the meeting."

"I will."

Chapter 3

The Houston Meeting

After Matt left the Quanda's house, he drove by Rice University and the Museum area, then spent some time looking at the old neighborhood where he had lived with Carol and the kids. At 11:20 he pulled up in front of the building at 800 Bell Street that housed the Petroleum Club. He turned his car over to the valet and took the elevator to the forty-third floor.

"I'm here to meet Mr. Kelly and Mr. Cernak," Matt said to the attractive woman at the desk.

"Yes sir, they're in the San Marcos room waiting for you. Follow me, please."

Matt walked behind her down the dark wood paneled hall with its plush carpets. When she opened the door, Matt saw two men across the room looking out the window at Houston's downtown. The taller man held a glass in his hand.

The men walked toward him around a table set for three in the middle of the room, and thanked the receptionist.

The larger man, about six feet four inches tall, appeared to weigh about two hundred and sixty pounds, most of it in the stomach. A full head of long gray hair, anchored by large sideburns, curled about the sides of his face and back. The gray suit he wore had a western cut to it. A large silver belt buckle poked out from his jacket with *Big Tex* written on it. Blond, almost invisible eyebrows topped his eyes while bags held up his baby blues. His Tony Lama boots completed an appearance that could have been a country western group publicity photo. "I'm Big Tex Cernak," he said in a hearty voice, extending a beefy hand that swallowed Matt's.

Billy Bob Kelly was a surprise too. Five foot four inches, his short black hair was graying around the temples. He had piercing black eyes and smooth olive skin. The gray Brooks Brothers suit and conservative striped tie make a sharp contrast with his partner.

"Hello," Billy Bob said in a well-modulated voice. "Thanks for driving down to meet with us."

"Have a drink." Big Tex ordered rather than asked. "Juan," he said to the waiter who had quietly entered the room, "bring me another bourbon and water and bring one for our guest."

"Thanks." Matt said slightly off balance.

"I'll have a Chardonnay," Billy Bob said.

Big Tex continued. "Juan, we want our guest to have the best we got so bring him and me the prime rib, medium rare, baked potato and all the fixins. We'll start with some French onion soup and a bottle of Frattoria di Vignamaggio,'96. Good year."

Matt wondered if Big Tex really knew one wine from another.

"For dessert," Big Tex said with a big smile on his

face, "we'll have the pecan ball with chocolate sauce. How does that sound to you, Matt?"

Matt, not normally reticent, but put on the defensive by Big Tex's whirlwind ordering said, "Sounds good." He could swear he heard Big Tex's accent change when he ordered the wine.

"You can handle it. I like to order because when you get someone new in here they have to read that damn big menu, half of it in some foreign language. Takes forever. They always end up with the prime rib anyway. Before those damn French oil companies stared moving here you could read the whole menu in a squiken."

"I'll have the chicken salad, dressing on the side and some iced tea. No soup for me." Billy Bob ordered quietly.

"Sit down, sit down. I need a couple of rolls before my next drink comes," Big Tex said. "Matt, let's be direct. Saves time. We've done our homework. You come highly recommended. Honest, diligent and all that stuff. Know your way around Kenya. What'd you actually do there?"

"Well, I negotiated one of the biggest oil exploration deals they ever had. Then a couple years later I came back and managed the operation."

Juan brought the soup, drinks and a bottle of red wine.

Big Tex sipped his drink and let his soup cool. Matt did the same.

"Interested in going back?" Big Tex asked.

"Could be. I liked the place."

"Well, we bought the maps and records from your

previous drilling from the National Oil Company. Our geologists want another go at it. We want you to get us a concession over your old area up in the Chalbi desert. Start with an option, maybe, so we can look around. Take a full concession if we get any encouragement. Think you can handle it?"

"Sure. What's the offer to the government?"

"We'll tell you that when we have an agreement with you that includes a confidentiality clause," Big Tex said. "Your pay won't be contingent on making a deal with the government so what do you care what the offer is?"

"I don't want to waste my time. Even if I'm paid I don't want to try to sell something that won't fly."

Billy Bob broke in. "It'll be a doable deal. We don't want to waste our time, either. We won't waste yours."

"Overseas exploration is a lot more expensive than drilling in the US," Matt said.

"Not as expensive for us as others. We're lean. Just Billy Bob and me plus a couple of secretaries and professional assistants. Everyone else, lawyers, geologists, drillers, you name it, work on a project basis. We don't have a lot of overhead, but we have lots of cash."

Juan returned with the meals and all the fixins Big Tex had ordered. The conversation halted as the dominant talker, Big Tex, attacked his food, then asked for his pecan ball. Matt was halfway through his meal when Big Tex put down his spoon and asked, "Whad'll you charge?"

Matt dug out the notes he made that morning and handed the list to Big Tex. Big Tex glanced at it, snorted and gave it to Billy Bob. Billy Bob read more slowly, then read it again out loud, "Each day or part day in Africa, $2,000. Each day or part day in the US, $1,000. Each day or part of day travel, $1,000. First class travel and air accommodations. Reimbursement of any and all direct and miscellaneous expenses incurred. Signing bonus $10,000. One million dollar life insurance policy. Medical coverage for anything not covered by my current policy if sickness or injury occurs while working under contract. Hold harmless agreement."

Billy Bob took a pen out of his pocket, made swift changes and gave the list back to Matt. Matt saw the following notations:

1. $2,000 changed to $1,000
2. $1,000 changed to $500
3. $1,000 changed to $500
4. First class travel "ok."
5. Reimbursement "ok"
6. Signing bonus, crossed out
7. Insurance policy crossed out
8. Medical coverage, crossed out
9. Hold harmless, crossed out

Billy Bob had added. "On the signature of an agreement with the Kenya Government over our area of interest, we will pay you a $100,000 bonus."

Billy Bob leaned forward and said, "We negotiate our deals. This negotiation just ended. Accept it?"

"I need the hold harmless."

"We'll think about it. What else?"

"Looks fine to me if your proposal to the government is reasonable. Like I said I don't want to go all that way, no matter what you pay me, if I don't have a chance to make a deal."

"Good. It's fair. Let's initial this list. I'll have our lawyers put the boiler plate around it and add something about you getting to put your two cents into the deal. We'll sign that."

"Fax it to me. If your proposal looks doable I'll come back next week."

"How soon can you leave?" Big Tex asked.

"Probably in two weeks."

"Great. Let's have a drink to celebrate."

"I'll have a bourbon and water," Matt said.

The one drink turned into another as Matt, Billy Bob and Big Tex searched their memories for mutual friends in the oil business. There were few and the men realized how distinct the international oil business was from domestic.

Finally Big Tex said, "See you next week. Take care."

Matt slipped as he stood. He realized how much he had had to drink. Carefully he shook hands with both men and left.

Billy Bob and Big Tex sat down. Big Tex said in a quieter voice, "Think he has a drinking problem?"

"No history of it. I think he'll do."

"Hope so. With his experience he can cut through the crap. Think your uncle knows what he's talking about?"

"He should. He was in the Counterintelligence Corps in Croatia at the end of World War II. Lots of strange things were going on. A lot of stuff taken by the Nazis was 'liberated' in various ways."

"Yeah, but did any of it end up in Kenya?"

"Don't know. That's what we hear. Let's play it out. If Stark can get us a concession, we get him out of there and take our time looking around the area. So we spend a couple of million. Cheaper than a well. If the rumors are true, it could be big bucks, tax free. Anyway you look at it, it'll be interesting. By the way, can you soft peddle that Big Tex act of yours. It's getting annoying. Save it for the investors. You sure as heck don't want to use it at your University of Chicago class reunion next year."

"You're right, Little Buddy," Big Tex said, slapping his partner on the back and almost knocking him down.

Chapter 4

Vienna

The airport in Frankfurt was as crowded as Matt had remembered, packed with both businessmen and tourists. As the central airport for industrial Germany, and a hub to the world for Lufthansa and most other international airlines, it throbbed with activity day and night. Fortunately, his membership in Lufthansa's Senator Club had not expired and he relaxed with a couple of drinks and a snack awaiting his connection to Nairobi.

He recalled being in the airport the day after the massacre in the Olympic Village in 1972. Now the bombing of the Nairobi embassy. What a violent world he sadly thought.

"Mr. Stark?" an attendant inquired.

"Yes."

"You have a call from the United States. You can take it over there."

Matt walked to the phone cubicle. "Stark here."

"Matt, Billy Bob in Houston. I told you we'd make money on this deal. Got a call from a lawyer in Vienna, Dr. Hans Wolffe. Says he represents a group of investors who've heard about our deal in Kenya and want to participate. I think we can promote our deal now. Talk to him. See if you can leverage him. Start out with them coming up with 66% to earn a third. See how it goes."

"Billy Bob, I've got a plane to Nairobi in an hour and appointments there the next couple of days."

"Don't worry. I'll rearrange the meetings. I've booked you on the next Lufthansa flight to Vienna. Look on the bright side, this way you can get a good night's sleep. Go see Wolffe. When you get a feel for their interest, or better still, an offer, call me. See if we can operate off someone else's cash."

Matt knew when he was on the short end. "Okay, I'll call you when I've got something to report."

The afternoon sky over Vienna was clear blue as the plane descended into to Schwechat Airport. Customs and immigration was a quick walk through. He avoided the crowd waiting for the express bus and took a cab for the twelve-mile ride to the city center. Instead of Hotel Sacher, where he usually stayed, he chose the historical Hotel Graben, a short walk from Wolffe's office in the Anker building at Graben and Dorothea Gasse. After completing the check-in with Germanic efficiency, he called Wolffe from his room and was immediately connected with the Doctor.

"Dr. Wolffe, this is Matt Stark. I'm told that you want to talk about our group's investment interest in Kenya."

"Yes, that's true," Dr. Wolffe said with a slight British accent.

"To be frank, I personally think that this discussion is premature," Matt said. "We haven't had any meaningful talks with the government and haven't fully evaluated the prospect. But my principals want me to meet with you so I'm here to meet."

"We don't share your view, Herr Stark. If you're just getting a seismic option, the true evaluation will come. As to the government discussions, we have great faith in your abilities. We wish to get in on the ground floor. We'll back that wish with cash. Please come to my office tomorrow morning at ten to meet my principals. We can discuss the matter in depth. You have the address I believe."

"Yes. I'll see you tomorrow at ten."

"Thank you, Herr Stark. I'm sorry that a previous engagement prevents me from inviting you for dinner. If you're not too tired, I might suggest you visit one of the heurige just outside the city and sample our white wine. The food is simple and substantial and the wine quite refreshing. In any event have a good evening and a restful slumber."

Matt had done the heurige bit in previous visits. It was fun but not alone and he didn't need a lot of food tonight. He ate a light supper in the hotel then walked over to Stephansplatz. On previous occasions, like a good tourist, he had gone as high as he could in the south tower of St. Stephen's Cathedral for its impressive view of the city and surrounding countryside. This time he satisfied himself with a walk around the Platz, wondering how Wolffe and his group had found out about the proposed deal in Kenya. They weren't oil people. What was their real interest? On the other hand, they wouldn't be the first non industry investors who tried to tag along on what they thought was a big bonanza. He'd know tomorrow.

Matt strolled down Rotenturm Strasse, round the Ring road and back toward his hotel. The night was pleasant, the streets crowded. Matt didn't notice the well-dressed gentleman who followed him at a discrete distance. As he neared his hotel Matt decided to join the Viennese in a nightcap. He sought out Demel's Konditori and he ordered a Sacher torte and a Doppel-mocha, a large cup of strong black coffee, and followed it with a schnapps.

Carol's favorite treat in Vienna had been the famous Sacher torte. If he didn't sleep it was worth it to bring back pleasant memories of their last trip here. He leisurely enjoyed his drink and watched couples stroll through the beautiful city as they had done. His thoughts of Carol drove out any concern he had about Wolffe. Back at the hotel his lack of sleep the night before and the schnapps overcame the coffee and he enjoyed a decent night's sleep.

Matt rose early and went to the exercise room, which seemed de riguer for all the better hotels now. He was no muscle man but after retiring, he and some of his buddies got a personal trainer, dropped a little weight and put some firmness in long unused muscles. This morning he did a short stint on the treadmill and a modified circuit on the Nautilus machines. He showered, ate a Continental breakfast and sat down in his room to outline a proposal he could make to Wolffe. He skimmed the sports scores in the "International Herald Tribune" to kill time. He left the hotel at 9:45 and arrived in Dr. Wolffe's office at 9:58. Nothing like Germanic punctuality.

"I'm Matt Stark. I have a ten o'clock appointment with Dr. Wolffe," he told the attractive blond receptionist.

"Yes," she said. "Dr. Wolffe and his associates are expecting you. Please follow me."

The simple gold plaque outside the ornate door listed five lawyers in the chambers of Dr. Wolffe. The paneled hallway reminded Matt of the Petroleum Club. The receptionist ushered him into a large corner office with an excellent view of St. Stephen's Cathedral.

Dr. Wolffe advanced across the well-appointed office to shake Matt's hand. "Good Morning, Herr Stark. Thank you for joining us." Wolffe, about five feet nine, looked like a lawyer with his black hair combed straight back to expose slight gray at the temples. Silver framed glasses added to the look. A well-cut blue suit that probably cost quite a few schillings completed the image. He looked to be in his fifties and fit enough to have been a strong football player in his youth.

"I'd like to introduce my colleagues, Dr. Konrad Rosenfeld and Herr Dieter Riba. Dr. Rosenfeld is the managing director of our investment group. Mr. Riba our chief financial officer. I am the avocate, or attorney as you would say."

Dr. Rosenfeld, tall and thin, appeared to be in his early fifties. His hairline had receded considerably, but Matt's attention was drawn to the man's deep-set dark eyes. Riba was about Wolffe's height but thicker in build. His full and flat face made him look more physical than cerebral. He appeared to be about ten years younger than Riba. If Wolffe had been a football player than Riba would have been a wrestler. The men were dressed in dark conservative suits that appeared to be less costly than the lawyer's. Both uttered simple greetings in accented English.

Rosenfeld's English had a sound of Italian about it but Matt couldn't be sure because of his terseness. Riba's accent sounded German.

Wolffe continued. "Our group consists of Austrian citizens who make substantial investments in high risk ventures. We, of course, anticipate high returns consistent with the risk if the venture succeeds. Here are our financial data and bank references."

"Frankly, your knowledge of our venture and interest is a surprise," Matt replied. "We're a small company and this is a small deal in the oil business. Furthermore, as I said on the phone, I think serious discussion is premature. But, I was instructed by my superiors to come listen to any reasonable proposal. Here I am. How'd you hear about this deal?"

Rosenfeld smiled, "Our group, has interests all over the world. One of our scouts overheard conversation at the Petroleum Club in Houston about your venture. Your presence here indicates our information had some basis in fact."

It would be hard not to overhear Billy Bob, Matt thought. "All right," Matt said, "but I need you to sign a non competition and confidentiality agreement before I can tell you the gist of our proposal."

"A reasonable approach," Wolffe agreed.

Matt took two copies of a signed two-page letter agreement with a map of their area of interest attached and handed them to Wolffe.

Wolffe glanced at the papers then back at Matt. "If you'll excuse us, we'll go into the conference room and review the document. In the meantime, I'll have coffee brought in unless you would prefer something else."

"Coffee will be fine. With cream please."

In the conference room the men quickly read the letter. "Pretty simple. No reason not to sign it," Wolffe said.

Rosenfeld and Riba were more interested in the map. They produced their own map and compared the land it outlined to the area of interest on Matt's map.

Rosenfeld said, "Their proposed area is what we were warned it would be, right next to North Horr. We'd better sign it so we can monitor the project."

Rosenfeld signed the letter and Wolffe witnessed his signature. "Let's have a cigarette and wait a little while so Stark doesn't think we rushed into this," Riba said.

Thirty minutes later the men returned with the signed agreement and kept a copy for themselves.

"All right," Matt said, "this is a small and risky deal. We want to take a seismic option over the land described in the agreement you just signed. We propose to pay a signature bonus of about $500,000 and a commitment to do seismic work over a two-year period and spend $2,000,000. What we don't spend goes to the government. At the end of two years we have the option to go into a five-year exploration period with the number of wells to be negotiated. Right now we're thinking of two at the most, with the right to back out after one. Of course, we'd be the operator. I think that's enough information right now. If it looks like we can make a deal we'll give full particulars in writing."

Wolffe nodded. "Rest assured that you can be the operator. We're investors, not drillers."

"We'd be interested in taking a fifty percent interest by paying half the expenses," Rosenfeld added.

"Mr. Rosenfeld, that proposal might be interesting to someone who has a hot prospect but no money. We have a prospect and money. If you want to participate you should think of paying half the cost until you've spent $1,250,000 to earn a 25% interest. Of course, the company's share of any oil found will be split 25/75 after the government takes its share."

"We can't agree to that," Rosenfeld countered. "It is too much leverage. I think that we have set a high and low for a potential deal. As you say, this is still early days and you have appointments with the Kenyan government. I suggest that we send a written proposal to your office in Houston outlining the parameters we've discussed. If the deal still looks possible we can get together to work out the final agreement."

"Fine, I'm flying back to Frankfurt this evening and getting an overnight flight to Nairobi tomorrow. I'll be in touch."

"Excellent. Thank you for coming, Mr. Stark," Wolffe held out his hand. Matt shook it, then Rosenfeld's and Riba's in turn.

"A pleasure to meet you. I look forward to our cooperation in this venture," Rosenfeld said.

Riba merely said, "Good-bye." It was the only thing he said at the meeting after the initial greeting but he had followed the discussion closely.

After Matt left the office, the three Austrians agreed that a deal seemed possible. Rosenfeld and Riba said their good-byes to Wolffe.

After they entered the elevator Riba turned to Rosenfeld and said in rapid German, "I told you they'd be too close. We have to do something."

"Relax, Riba, everything's under control. We'll watch them."

"That's not enough. I want to stop the project now."

"Riba, don't do anything, and that's an order," Rosenfeld said curtly. "Any action will only draw unwanted attention to us. Your hot-headedness has caused us enough problems already. One more incident and you're finished."

"Don't order me around, Colonel. I'll do what's best for the cause." When the elevator doors opened Riba strode off quickly and darted through the lobby doors. Rosenfeld caught up with him two blocks down the strasse.

"In here," he snapped, pointing into one of the ubiquitous coffee houses. Once seated in a remote corner with their coffee in front of them Rosenfeld began. "Party discipline, Riba. Have you ever heard of it? You lost your attempt to take over. Drop it. Quit causing trouble."

Riba sneered. "Look Rosenfed, you can't make correct decisions for the cause. You're biased. Your doddering parents are among the old party members we're wasting good money on to feed. We need that money for our action groups. We get more votes each election. Young people are with us. Soon we'll be able to get rid of the guest workers and other vermin. Quit wasting the money on the old and feeble. Their day is past. They're finished."

"The money was taken to support everyone who was loyal, especially those who couldn't get out of Europe. They never had decent jobs again. Not every one was a Waldheim."

"No. The money belongs to the cause. It's more important than a few pensioners."

"Drop it, Riba. Forget about Stark, too. We'll watch him. He won't find anything. If he gets too close we will handle him like the others who poked around in the desert."

"Stop him now before he gets near the mission and complicates things," Riba warned as he rose. "Or I will."

A few seconds later Rosenfeld went out the door and followed slowly after Riba. Riba walked to his car and threw his suit coat and tie into the back seat. He put on a three-quarter length black leather jacket and matching black cap. It was a short walk to Matt's hotel.

The meeting in Wolffe's office had lasted less than sixty minutes. Matt strolled back to his hotel and at noon called Houston to catch anyone who had come in early. He got no answer and recorded a message for Billy Bob saying that Wolffe's people looked responsible and serious. He suggested Houston check on their financial reliability. After he hung up he still wondered how Wolffe's group had heard about them and why they were interested in a longshot investment in the Kenyan desert. Surely there were a lot more interesting investments floating around the Wiener Bourse.

He read some of his LaCarré novel, then decided on

one more walk around the Ringstrasse and a stop for lunch. As he passed through the lobby, Matt didn't notice the man in a three-quarter length black leather jacket and matching hat who put down his newspaper and followed him out the door. Riba appreciated Matt's leisurely pace.

Matt strolled to Kartnerstrasse and down Kartner to the Ring enjoying the old buildings of Vienna. He turned into the Cafe Schwarzenberg, took a table near the window and ordered a beer, an Obstler schnapps and some wurst. After he finished eating he ordered Driezner mit Schlag, coffee with cream and settled in to watch the people pass.

When Matt stopped for lunch, Riba took a seat at a konditori across the way and ordered coffee. He paid for it immediately so he could move when his target moved. He appeared to be reading a copy of "Der Standard" while watching Matt but in reality, he was turning over the situation in his mind again and again and growing more agitated. He reaffirmed to himself that Rosenfeld was a weak fool and that he should handle the situation himself, and the sooner the better.

While Matt had not noticed Riba, neither had Riba noticed that he was under surveillance by a three-person team, an elderly gentleman in a business suit, a leather-jacketed man in his twenties and a middle-aged Viennese woman doing some window shopping. They followed standard surveillance technique, one was ahead of Riba, one behind and one across the street at all times.

Matt gathered his change and walked casually back to the hotel. Riba followed. When Matt entered his hotel Riba, waited a few seconds, then went into the lobby just in time to see Matt enter the elevator. When the sign indicated the elevator had stopped at Matt's floor Riba turned and went back out the front door.

Riba walked to the end of the building, then alongside until he reached a small alleyway in the back. As he entered the alley one of his followers made a quick cell phone call. Riba eased down the alley looking for an entry to the hotel, trying to ignore the smells from the garbage. He reached a door marked "deliveries" and started to turn the handle. A voice cracked from behind him.

"What are you doing Riba?"

Riba spun around. "What I told you, Colonel. Protecting our interests. We can't let this fool go mucking around."

"You'll interfere more than he will if you do anything that draws attention to us. We can take care of it in the desert."

"You're wrong," Riba said. He pulled a Beretta from inside his jacket. "Move on. Let me do my job."

Two shots came from Rosenfeld's coat pocket. The first hit Riba in the stomach and the second in the right shoulder spinning him sideways. Riba fell on his right side, his weapon in his hand under him. Rosenfeld saw a figure running toward them from the far end of the alley. He turned and fled. As Rosenfeld ran, the approaching man began to walk cautiously toward the bleeding figure. Keeping his gun aimed at Riba he felt his throat with his other hand and found a pulse.

"Riba?"

A moan came from injured man's throat.

"Remember Jasenovac?" he said softly. The red headed man then turned Riba fully on his face and held him there while he groped for the Beretta. When he finally got it he held the muzzle against the back of Riba's skull and fired. "For justice." He pulled Riba partly up by one shoulder, threw the gun under him and walked slowly out of the alley.

03   03   03

Matt paid his bill and left the hotel for his seven p.m. flight to Frankfurt. When he got to the Austrian Air counter to check in the clerk said, "One moment, Herr Stark, I believe there is a message for you." The man disappeared into the back room and came out holding a white envelope. He checked Stark's name again against the name on the envelope and handed it to him with a dramatic flourish. At that moment, two men in the waiting area rose from their seats and positioned themselves between Matt and the exit. Matt opened the envelope. The note inside requested him to go to the security office on the second floor of main building.

"May I have my boarding pass?" Matt asked.

The man shook his head. "Sorry, but I've been instructed to wait until you clear security."

Perplexed, Matt saw no alternative so he took the elevator to the second floor. The two men joined him on the elevator.

Matt exited at the second floor and found the door marked "Security." He entered and introduced himself to the male clerk. "I'm Matt Stark. Somebody here wants to see me."

"Yes, Mr. Stark. Go right in. The Inspector is expecting you."

Still puzzled Matt entered. "What's going on?" he said to the two men in the room. "I'm going to miss my plane. This better be important."

The older man answered. "I apologize, Mr. Stark. This is important. I'm Inspector Otto Krueger of the Bundes Polizei. I have a couple of questions to ask you. You'll not miss your connection unless absolutely necessary. As back-up we have booked you on another flight in an hour."

Although Krueger smiled, he had a no nonsense look about him. The strict appearance was reinforced by his black leather trench coat.

"Wait a minute," Matt said. "This looks pretty serious to me. I'm not talking to anyone until I call my embassy."

"Ah, yes, rightly so," Krueger said. "Excuse my bad manners. I'd like to introduce you to Sean Casey of the US Consulate in Vienna."

Casey, in his early thirties, had an open face set off by red hair and freckles. He extended his right hand to greet Matt and held out his credentials with his left. After some fumbling, Matt looked at a photo ID that identified Casey as an assistant consul of the United States of America. He looked more like a college sophomore.

"Well, this looks official. What's going on?" Matt asked.

"We'd like you to look at some pictures and tell us if you know these people. We asked Mr. Casey to be here so there would be no delay if you requested help. Hopefully, we can all be on our way shortly."

"All right. I know few people in Vienna but I'll do what I can. Can't you tell me more?"

"In a moment." Krueger spread five head shots of men in business suits on the table. "Please look at these and tell us if you know any of them and whatever you know about them."

Matt looked at the pictures and immediately recognized Rosenfeld and Riba.

"Yes, I met these two men at a meeting this morning at Dr. Hans Wolffe's office here in Vienna. I hadn't seen them before nor since. I don't know the other three."

"We are familiar with Dr. Wolffe. What was the meeting about?" Krueger asked.

"Some Americans I represent are proposing to enter into an oil exploration deal in Kenya. A group Wolffe represents wants to buy into the venture." Matt gave them a summary of the discussion.

"Where in Kenya?"

"The Chalbi desert in the north of Kenya."

"What did this man have to do with this?" Krueger asked, pointing to Riba's picture.

"He was introduced as the financial officer of the group but he didn't say anything. Dr. Wolffe can confirm all this."

"He already has to some extent. We plan to talk to him again, but as you were leaving the country we thought we should talk to you first."

"You still haven't told me what this all about."

"First a couple more questions, Mr. Stark. Were there

44

any arguments in the meeting between Riba and you or Riba and anyone?

"No, like I said, Riba hardly spoke except to say hello and good-bye."

"Did you notice any signs of any animosity?"

"No. Now can you answer my question?"

"Partially, Riba's body was found in the alley behind your hotel about three hours ago. He had been shot, once in the back of the head, execution style. Like an American gangland slaying."

"Or like a Gestapo killing," Casey interjected.

Krueger glanced quickly to Casey but then asked Matt, "Did you shoot him, Herr Stark?"

"My God, no."

"Where were you this afternoon?"

"Just walking the streets, sightseeing."

"Anybody see you?"

"Lots of people but I don't know any of them."

"Okay, please sit down and write out where you walked and when. Give me your extra passport photo. We'll check out your story."

"I just met the man," Matt protested. "Why are you interested in me?"

"You were one of the last people to see him alive. Riba had a Beretta and a piece of paper with your room number on it. Do you know why?"

Shaken, Matt sank into a chair. "I don't know. What's going on?"

"We don't know either. We'll find out."

"Are you going to hold me? I'd like to call my office."

"Just a moment, Mr. Stark, until I confer with Mr. Casey."

☳ ☳ ☳

Casey and Krueger went to the next room. "Well, what do you think?" Krueger asked.

"I don't think he knows a thing. We know he didn't kill Riba because we had a tail on him and Riba after the meeting. He's clean as the new fallen snow," Casey said.

"No need to let him know that. I'll let him go to Kenya and you take him over. I'll investigate the murder here."

"Right, we'll pick him up in Kenya. What happened to your people following Riba?"

"He lost them. Riba went in and out of a few stores checking for a tail. One of our people followed him in. Then Riba sat down to try on shoes. Our guy thought he would be there for a while and went to the bathroom. When he got back Riba was gone. The clerk said Riba just sat down, took one shoe off, put it back on and took off. He must have gone out a service exit because he didn't come back out the front door."

"My God, that trick is out of Surveillance 101 at intelligence school."

"Guess he flunked it."

"Let's go tell Stark he can go."

They reentered the office.

"Mr. Stark," Krueger said," I see no indication at this time that you are involved in this matter so you are free to go. There is an airline representative outside who will assist you in getting the next flight to Frankfurt. Please write down where we can get hold of you for the next month in case we want to talk to you some more. Here are our cards. We can be reached anytime. If you think of anything, anything at all that can help, call me. By the way, don't contact Dr. Wolffe again until you talk to me."

Irritated, puzzled, but happy to be free to go, Matt nodded curtly. "Fine. Good-bye Inspector. Good-bye Mr. Casey."

The airline representative hustled Matt through the procedures and on to the plane. Before long he found himself back in the Senator Lounge in Frankfurt. Still shaken and puzzled over his strange encounter, he decided to call Casey to see if he could find out more about what was going on before he talked to Houston. He placed the call with the multilingual operator in the lounge to the US Embassy in Vienna. He was connected with the night duty officer.

"I'd like to talk to Assistant Consul Sean Casey or if he not around leave a message."

"Sorry, sir, there is no Sean Casey at the Embassy."

"He's at the Consulate."

"Sorry, he'd still be on the roster I have. I see no such listing. Besides, I've been here two years and don't recall anyone by that name."

"I met him this afternoon. He showed me his credentials."

"Sorry, sir. Unfortunately lots of people try to pass themselves off as officials to impress others."

"This wasn't that type of situation."

"Well, I can't help you further. Sorry."

The attendant appeared. "Herr Stark, that's the last boarding call for your flight."

Stark hung up the phone and walked toward his gate more concerned than before.

Chapter 5

Northern Ireland

Lena Daly edged sideways through the crowd streaming out of ten o'clock mass at St. Columba's. If she could get out of the line led by her mother and two sisters she wouldn't have to tell Monsignor O'Brien what a fine sermon he had preached. Actually, she thought it was dreadful. Besides, she didn't like him reminding everyone the Civil Rights parade that afternoon wasn't authorized by the authorities.

Of course they wouldn't authorize a parade protesting internment laws that let them imprison people without trial. Lots of parades that weren't authorized had been held and nothing much came of it.

Lena popped her chunky frame through the crowded door and on to the top step. She searched the crowd of gossipers for Bridget Kelly's red head, much brighter than her own auburn hair. She finally spotted her chum at the end of the square talking to two boys.

Lena and Bridget had left school together last year. They were bright enough but like most school leavers had not gone on to college, nor were they particularly interested in more school. They were, however, interested in boys, especially the two with Bridget.

Work was not easy to come by in Derry, especially if you were a Catholic. Lena's Dad and brothers had no steady work. But one of Bridget's relatives had helped the girls get part-time jobs in Bewley's Cafe setting out the food for the cafeteria line and cleaning off tables. Bewley's headquarters was in Dublin so they were more open to hiring Catholics. The job wasn't much but it brought money into the household that Lena's mother, Mary, tried to maintain for five children and their mostly unemployed father. It also paid for Lena's cigarettes.

"Hi, Bridget, Liam, Peter. What are you fussing about?"

"I want Peter to take me to the movies this afternoon like he promised but he wants to march in that awful parade." Bridget pouted.

"No, I didn't promise. Besides we can go to the movies another time. The parade is only today."

"Blather, there's some type of demo all the time, for all the good they do." Lena said. "Besides you and your hooligan buddies' go to Aggro corner almost every afternoon and throw stones at the Brits." Bridget used the common nickname for the corner of Peters Street and Rossville where the demolished buildings gave unemployed young men a vacant place to gather.

"There should be stone throwing until the Brits get their soldiers out of here. Especially the paratroopers. They're a fecking nasty lot," Peter added

"Yeah, a bunch of thugs in uniform." Liam said.

"Monsignor O'Brien said to keep it peaceful." Lena reminded them to show she had heard a least part of what the priest had said.

"What's your Da say?" Liam asked Lena. "I hear he's a member of the Citizen's Defense Association. They're a tough lot."

"He's not a member," Lena protested.

"Come with us," Peter pleaded with the two girls. "It's just a lark. Be lots of women and kids, some of them in their prams. A nice Sunday stroll and we can hoot at the troops."

"No," Lena said

"I'll tell you what," Bridget said. "We'll come down to Rossville near the end of the parade and you can take us for a treat after."

"Fine then," Liam said. "We'll walk on the outside of the marchers so you can see us."

On that understanding the couples split. Lena and Bridget stopped for a coffee and a cigarette on the way home.

"Liam's really cute." Lena said.

"You've got a crush on him."

"Of course I do. But he thinks I'm a little girl."

"No, he doesn't. Not the way he looks at your chest. You've got to be a little more aggressive."

"I couldn't do that."

"You better do something this afternoon or he's going to spend all his time with Sheila."

"That slut?"

"Exactly."

At 3:30 the girls walked down Peters Street to the corner of Rossville. At 3:45, when they arrived at curbside, the parade had swelled as watchers from the curb joined the marchers. It was a festive crowd. The sun shone. Blue and White civil rights banners flew over the crowd. Boys and girls darted around their parents. The forecasted babies in prams joined the predominately male marchers.

Lena and Bridget noticed the paraders grew quieter as they neared Aggro corner and the parade marshals tried to turn them right onto Rossville towards the proposed rally area at Free Derry Corner. However, a large group, led by young men, continued down Peters street toward Barrier 14, one of the many barriers erected by the British to limit access from Bogside into the City center. Liam and Peter were in that group.

The Royal Green Jackets, supported by a water cannon, manned Barrier 14 today. Hidden from sight, the British had Saracen Armored Personnel carriers, called Pigs by the locals, at the ready. Each Pig contained a group of paratroopers in their jump helmets and red berets. Snipers sat quietly in the second floors of houses on either side of the barrier.

"Do you see Liam or Peter?" Lena asked.

"Not yet."

"I told him this side of the street. Could they screw that up?"

"Sure."

Liam and Peter arrived with the crowd at the barricade where the mob pushed them against the barbed wire. Others began taunting the troops and throwing stones. An RUC, Royal Ulster Constabulary, police inspector gave the official notice through a loudspeaker. "This assembly may lead to a breach of the peace. You are to disperse immediately."

The crowd responded by yelling louder and throwing more stones. The water cannon fired its purple dyed water. A gas canister bounced in front of the crowd. The demonstrators backed off but reformed. Now the majority of the demonstrators in front of the barricade were young men. When this was reported to the command center the order went out to enforce the plan to arrest the hooligans. In response, the Pigs carrying the paratroopers burst through the barrier and into Rossville Street.

Lena and Bridget heard the shouts from down the street. Looking toward the noise they saw people, men, women and children running toward them.

"Run! It's pepper gas!" someone shouted.

"They're shooting!"

"Rubber bullets?" a bystander asked.

"No, real ones!" came the answer.

The armored vehicles moved a hundred yards down the street and stopped. Troops poured from the back and took positions facing the crowd. More sounds of weapons firing exploded. The running crowd grew in size and speed. People yelled. People ran. Some were jumped over or stepped on. Many coughed and gasped from the gas. The purple dye gave those it came into contact with a ghoulish appearance. The swirling gas attacked and stung eyes and throats, including Lena's and Bridget's. They found themselves trapped by the running crowd and they huddled in a small courtyard to avoid being trampled. Four men carried a young man into the courtyard and lay him down.

"Call the paramedics! Call an ambulance!" one of the

men shouted. Blood flowed from the youth's nose and mouth, drenching his shirt.

"It's Liam!" Lena shrieked. She leaped to her feet.

"No, it's not," Bridget said. "Let's go. The soldiers are following the crowd." She pulled hard on Lena dragging her toward the street.

A panicked voice came from the house. "There's no phone here!" Cursing, the men picked up the bleeding boy and started back into the street. Bridget pulled Lena out of the courtyard. The panic stricken mob pushed and shoved them further down Rossville. Bridget dragged Lena into the first side street they came upon. Lena, now crying hysterically, dropped to her knees. Bridget knelt beside her and they crawled behind a coal lorry as more people flooded into the side street.

Two men, carrying another bloody body, hurried past them. Lena was shaking uncontrollably, her breath coming with great sobs. Bridget got out her handkerchief and dug Lena's out of her pocket. More shots and screaming filled the air. They covered their faces and moved down the side street away from the turmoil.

At Abbey Park they ran into an alley. A door opened and a woman said, "Come in."

Bridget steered the crying Lena into the open doorway which was shut quickly behind them.

"Lay your friend down on the couch," the woman said to Bridget. "I'll get some wet cloths and water." The woman quickly returned and gave a washcloth to Bridget, who kept herself under control despite the awful experience. She began wiping down her face and exposed skin. Bridget did the same for Lena. Eventually the woman and the girl calmed Lena.

"It's quieter outside now," the woman said. "Apparently the main activity is back by Rossville. You can leave now if you wish."

"Thank you. I think I can get her home now."

With Lena leaning on her, Bridget escorted her friend by side streets to her home.

"Jesus, Mary and Joseph!" Mary, Lena's mother exclaimed as they came through the door. "What happened?"

"The Brits came firing at the crowd. We got stampeded and gassed. A boy got shot and Lena thinks it's Liam. She went off on me."

"Was it Liam?"

"I don't know."

"Come, Lena. Lay down in the bedroom. I'll get you something."

Mary searched her medicine cabinet and found sedatives that had been prescribed for her a year or so ago.

"Here, take these. They'll help you sleep. I'll call the doctor later." Eventually the girl fell asleep.

"Kevin," Mary said to her son. "Take Bridget home. God knows she's had a terrible time her own self. God bless you, Bridget and take care."

"What? Where?" Lena awakened in her bed from her drugged sleep. It all came back: the press of bodies; the acrid smell of gas; the bloody boy. Lena screamed.

Mary rushed in from the kitchen. She had been going over the news in the morning paper and drinking tea with the downstairs neighbor Sheila Flynn. She had dreaded

Lena's waking. By now the women had pieced together the story from the papers and the radio. Thirteen people killed and many more wounded when the British army opened fire with live ammunition on the crowd. The Bogside area was inflamed. The town was on the verge of armed warfare. The authorities and the church called for calm. All Mary was concerned about was the sobbing child in her arms and how she would tell her Liam was dead.

"Darlin', darlin'," she said as she stroked Lena's hair and rocked her. "Dr. Egan said to call when you woke up. He'll be here shortly. Let me get you some tea."

Lena, in drugged passivity, lay back on the bed and stared at the ceiling.

Dr. Egan finished his examination and came out to the two women. "She's resting. Nothing physical I can find. She's suffering shock and stress. Only time can cure her. She might need some therapy. Let's wait and see. I'll leave a prescription for sedatives. Make her rest but I want her up and doing normal things as soon as possible. Call when you need me."

"Don't go yet. I want you here when I tell her that Liam's dead."

Mary went into the room and delivered her message. Lena groaned and fainted.

ଔ   ଔ   ଔ

Three weeks later, Lena was able to do small chores around the house but didn't go back to her old job. She had trouble sleeping through the night without medication. Detached and dazed, she spent most of her time sitting in her room looking at the wall. Visits from her friends upset her. Unable to attend Liam's funeral she sat at home. She didn't want to know anything about it. She talked only to her family.

"Lena, Uncle Colin is here from Belfast. He wants to say hello. All right?"

"All right, Mother."

Uncle Colin, Mary's brother, was a traveling salesman based in Belfast. His job let him travel freely in the north and he sometimes went south to the Republic.

"Hello, Lena. I'm very sorry about your troubles. Filthy, Brits. They won't ever be satisfied. Terrible about your friend."

Lena put her handkerchief to her eyes but didn't cry. "Thank you."

"I've business in the town so I thought I'd drop in."

"How are Mary Ann and Clare?"

"Fine as any lasses in Belfast. They send their prayers and they want you to come and visit them."

"Thank them but I can't leave."

"Lena, your mother asked me to come. Dr. Egan says you should get away. Come to Belfast. Live with us. Being with a couple of girls near your own age will help. We'd love to have you."

"I'll never forget what happened."

"No, you won't ever forget it, but you can't live in that moment forever. You've got to go on."

Eventually everyone convinced the distressed Lena to live with her cousins in Belfast for a bit.

og   og   og

Lena's physical symptoms eased as she shared time with her cousins but her hatred for Liam's murderers grew. More and more evidence came to the front that the British soldiers had not been fired upon and that they ran amok, shooting indiscriminately. Those who made it their business to know such things in Catholic Belfast knew about her experience. Eventually, without her taking note of it, she was befriended by a number of people who were sympathetic with the Real IRA, a small radical offshoot of the IRA.

One evening at the local pub one of the young men she had met signaled her over.

"Lena, I want you to meet a mate of mine. Mick, this is Lena. Lena, Mick."

"Sit for a minute, Lena," Mick said as he motioned her to a seat.

Lena sat out of curiosity. She wondered what the balding thirtyish man would want. She would have been surprised to know that the unthreatening looking Mick was listed by British intelligence as a Real IRA terrorist. The two men he had been visiting with left.

"I hear that a good friend of yours was killed by the Brits on Bloody Sunday."

"I don't want to talk about it," Lena said as she pushed back her chair.

"Wait. We're your friends. We're looking for good people who are motivated. We think you're one of them."

"Who's we?"

"Let's leave that aside for now. Would you like to honor Liam's life?"

"Yes. With all my heart."

"We can help you. Meet me tomorrow at this address and I'll lay out the particulars." He handed her a piece of paper with an address on it and left.

The next week, Lena found herself in the Fiumiciano airport in Rome awaiting the next Alitalia flight to Tripoli, Libya.

೧ ೧ ೧

"Run, Lena, run. It's only another hundred yards."

"Squeeze the trigger, Lena. Squeeze, don't jerk. Try it again."

"All right. All of you crawl on your stomach. The machine gun is set to fire three feet off the ground. Keep down and you won't be hurt. When you come to the barbed wire turn on your back, hold the wire up and wriggle under. Start when I blow the whistle."

He nodded to Lena, "Good run, Lena. A new personal best."

೧ ೧ ೧

A few weeks later, Lena was living quietly with Helen, a fellow recruit, in an apartment in Belfast and clerking in a grocery store. One day Mick visited her at the apartment. "Lena, you know Eamon. Small town southwest of here?"

"I've heard of it. Never been there."

"That's okay. We've got a little job for you and Helen. The town is a republican town. Our organization

59

there is strong. We get a lot of 'voluntary' contributions from the merchants."

"So."

"One of the merchants told us he's not going to support us anymore."

"Can't you get along without him?"

"Sure but it's a bad idea. He's talking it up among the other business owners. Says that he wants the British out but we're the wrong way to go."

"And?"

"We need to give a little warning. We want you to leave a little souvenir in his shop. Get him back in line so to say."

"I won't deliberately harm anyone."

"No, no. Nothing like that. Just a scare. A little property damage. His store closes early on Thursday night so he can go to the Holy Name meeting at his church. No one'll be in the shop. We give a code warning to the RUC so they can clear the area. A scare is all we're after."

"What's the plan?"

"Right you are then. Go with Tom. He'll brief you and Helen."

At five thirty in the evening the following Thursday, Lena and Helen entered a bookstore on South High Street a half block south of Church Street, the main thoroughfare in the little town. The shopkeeper and his clerk were checking out customers and otherwise getting ready for the six o'clock closing. Lena walked to the shelves nearest the front window and took a Bible from the display in the window itself. She leafed through it and replaced it. With a glance to confirm the checkouts were still going on, she removed a similar Bible from her bag and placed it in the display window. Lena and Helen left, but not too quickly. They went to the car given to them for the assignment and headed for Belfast. They had been in the store less than five minutes.

ભ   ભ   ભ

The phone woke the policeman who had been dozing at the end of his shift in the RUC office.

"Good evening, Officer Cody. How are you this fine evening?"

"Who's this?"

"Never mind. Listen closely. This is a code blue warning. A bomb is set to go off at six thirty in the South High Street. Code blue. Do your job."

Cody, shocked into alertness, knew what a code blue warning was but never expected to receive one. He pushed the emergency button that alerted the RUC bomb unit in Belfast and all the cruising patrol cars. A second button rang all the phones and cell phones of off duty officers. He ran into the chief's office. "There is a code blue for North High Street. I've alerted the force."

"Block off North High Street for three blocks from Church to Murphy. Get everyone out of there. Everyone knows the drill. You and Mullin stay here. Keep me advised if anything else come in. Get the dogs down there. I'm on my way."

ભ   ભ   ભ

Orla and John had finished a pint at their local after finishing their shopping. As they left the pub they saw a commotion two blocks away. "What's going on down the street?" Orla asked.

"Don't know. Let's go see."

They walked up to the back of the crowd and saw the barricade.

"What's about?" he asked the officer standing there.

"Bomb warning. We cleared everybody out and are searching. Of course everyone stands here behind the barricade to see what's going on. You should move along."

"We will. Just came to see the fuss."

"John, come here. I want to show you something. I think I saw a good gift for Brian's Confirmation."

Orla lead John to the bookstore window. They were looking at the display of Bibles when the bomb exploded. Glass and bits of brick and metal flew in all directions. The front of the store looked like it had been hit with a massive wrecking ball. A dozen people behind the barricade were injured by the hail of glass and jagged pieces of metal and stone.

John and Orla had closed caskets at their wake. Even with stitching, the faces were almost unrecognizable.

ೞ ೞ ೞ

"You lied to me! You lied to me!" Lena screamed as she threw the newspaper into Mick's face. "You told me no casualties. You bastard!"

"Lena, wait! Wait!" Mick grabbed her. "It wasn't our

fault. The stupid RUC misunderstood us. They herded the people toward the bombsite on South High Street. We did what we could."

"No you didn't. You don't have to set off bombs at all."

"It's a war, Lena. England's an occupying power. Ask the soldiers who shot Liam."

"I've been a fool. This isn't going to bring Liam back."

"Calm down, Lena."

"I'm calm. You're no better than the Brits. Bloody, fecking, murdering bastards. You can all go to hell!" Lena hit Mick across the mouth and ran from the room. She got into the car the group had given her and started to wonder if she could avoid both the IRA and the RUC and get safely to Dublin.

Chapter 6

Arrival in Nairobi

Matt woke to an offer of juices by the attendant. He took orange juice. The sugar helped him get out of the groggy sensation he always had when he woke up on a plane. He hated the sticky feeling from sleeping in his clothes. As soon as he could, he went into the lavatory, brushed his teeth and shaved. That made him feel better.

He made his way back to his seat to wait for breakfast. After seeing his fellow passengers he thought that sometime he would have to travel as informally as they did, wearing t-shirts, blue jeans, shorts, and track suits. Despite the prospect of comfort, he still felt he was treated better with a jacket, preferably blue, and tie. Just an old habit. Anyway, he needed the pocket in the jacket to hold his passport he rationalized.

He enjoyed the breakfast of bacon, scrambled eggs, roll, butter, jelly, and coffee. It reminded him of Sunday morning breakfasts at home before Carol died. Matt looked out the window.

As the sun rose in the sky, Matt saw the vast expanse of the Sudan. Somewhere down there Muslims were still fighting Christians as they had been for centuries. Matt tried to jerk himself back to the present and be positive. He thought he had made peace with Carol's death but he had to keep it in hand or he'd find himself struggling with a flood of negative thoughts. She wouldn't have wanted that.

For the first time since he left Texas he questioned his reasons for accepting this mission. Was he running away from living without Carol and everyone who offered help? He heard on the radio before he left home that people his age could expect to live another twenty years. Long enough to see his grandchildren in and out of college. Just hope I don't have to pay for it, he thought.

He turned his attention back to the vast, unending vista of Africa below him. Sometimes it appeared bleak brown and sometimes green. At this height you saw nothing but lifeless flat terrain for hours. But on the ground, the earth rose and fell, especially the Rift Valley that ran from Egypt down through Kenya. In some spots it teemed with life. Too much human life in many areas.

The steward passed out landing cards and Matt dug around for his pen. Lake Turkana appeared briefly on the right as the plane passed into Kenyan air space. The passengers on the other side of the plane would be able to see Mount Kenya, snow and all. According to the Kikuyus, God lived on Mount Kenya. Why not?

Matt gathered up his belongings as the plane started the long gradual descent into Jomo Kennyatta Airport, named after the first president of Kenya, a freedom fighter before the term was a popular one. The automatically controlled landing was uneventful. The plane pulled up to its unloading gate and the aisles, even in first class, bustled with people competing to get their luggage out of the overhead bins.

Matt always felt the arrival at Kennyatta Airport was great training for Kenya and Africa. If you stayed calm and weren't in a hurry, you'd get your bags, or your business done in due time. Matt came off the plane, walked into the central corridor that connected the various gates and down the steps into the vast, jammed baggage area. Although enormous, Matt found the area more crowded since the introduction of wide bodied planes and scheduling that landed all of the airlines from Europe within a few early morning hours.

Passengers of all colors turned the baggage area into a kaleidoscope of colors, their skin accented by the diverse colors and styles of the clothing: business suits, serious dresses, casual dresses, slacks, shorts, safari suits, warm up suits, saris and t-shirts. White clothing predominated but a plethora of yellow, red, blue, black and orange created contrast amid the sea of white. Voices rose in the classic Babel of Swahili, Italian, French, German, Spanish, Danish with an English overlay in many accents.

Matt stood off to one side and kept an eye on the carousel where the Lufthansa bags were supposed to come. Finally his arrived, hidden among all the hundreds of packages and bundles people were bringing back home. He grabbed his and looked for a line with the fewest Kenyans. It wasn't prejudice that dictated this choice but practicality as he knew that homecoming Kenyans got a more serious grilling from the customs officers than the tourists. Their trolleys were usually loaded down with items unavailable or unduly pricey here in the home country and, therefore, took longer to clear.

Matt usually didn't have a problem and today was no exception. When Matt arrived at the front of the line the inspector looked at his passport and papers and into his briefcase.

"Welcome to Kenya. How long will you be staying?"

"Just a few days. Visiting some old friends." Matt had a tourist visa. It was much easier to obtain than the business visa and was always used by businessmen planning a short stay. The government didn't seem to mind.

"Then you've been here before?"

"Yes, I lived here at one time."

"Welcome back," she said in her melodic Kenyan-English accent.

He had heard all the stories of expatriates being unduly delayed or being solicited for bribes directly or indirectly by customs people. It had never happened to him in Kenya. He couldn't say the same of other African countries. In fact he adopted a practice of carrying certain small items in his briefcase in case the customs official might like an extra lighter or pen.

Matt thanked the customs officer, picked up his briefcase and suitcases and walked through the exit doors. Once through those doors, he felt truly back in Kenya. He blended into the hundreds of people of all sizes and shades, waiting for relatives, friends and customers to come out. It was even more crowded than inside.

Above the conversational drone rose the call of the drivers looking for customers. Hands snatched to carry his bag to the taxi they drove or touted for. Forty or fifty signs with the names of safari companies or tourists on them were held high to attract the visitor with a prearranged ride.

Matt edged his way through the crowd as best he could. He angled off to the right where the taxis of the Kenatco Company parked. The regular taxis queued at the front exit and tried to cram as many people in as they could. What the owner of Kenatco taxis paid, and to whom, to get to use the side entrance Matt could not guess but he was sure that it paid a good return.

Matt got to the side exit with his bags still in his hands. A Kenyan in coat and tie asked where he was going.

"The Norfolk," he said, naming the traditional old hotel west of the downtown area.

The Norfolk was built in the early days to cater to the white settlers on the way to their farms in the highlands or when they came into town for business or celebrations.

The Kenyan raised his arm. An older but well polished gray Mercedes Benz backed out of a parking slot and came to a stop in front of him. The driver quickly stowed his bags in the trunk. Matt gave the destination to the driver and the car moved out of the car park and on to Uhuru, Swahili for *Independence Road*, and headed for Nairobi.

"Welcome. My name is Joseph. Is this your first time in Kenya, Bwana?"

"No. I've visited here many times. I lived here for three years once."

"Welcome back. I hope that we haven't changed too

much since you were here. If you need a driver while you are here I will give you a card. Please call for me."

"Thanks. How long have you been driving?"

"For Kenatco, about ten years. Before that I drove for the Managing Director of a French Company until they closed their operation."

"Do you speak French?"

"Un petite. They sent me to the French Alliance to study and some of it sunk in. Most Kenyans speak English, Swahili and their tribal language so we can sometimes pick up a fourth or fifth language. And you, Bwana?"

"I do a good version of American English. I took some Swahili lessons while I was here but everybody speaks English so I was spoiled."

Matt leaned back in his seat and looked at the skyline of the city. The white highrise circular conference center and the other tall office buildings reminded him more of Europe than Africa. The driver expertly maneuvered through the roundabout intersections of Haile Selassie Avenue and Kenyatta Avenue that allowed the busy traffic to move with some semblance of smoothness. Matt looked down Kenyatta Avenue with its eight lanes of traffic divided by two green belts. The palm trees gave shade to the cars parked at an angle while their owners conducted business in the private and government offices that lined the street.

At University Way, the driver circled past the local synagogue, past Nairobi University on the left, and turned onto Harry Thuku Road. The taxi passed a dozen zebra striped minivans loading and unloading tourists and pulled into the unloading area for the historic Norfolk Hotel. The six-feet-four-inch, two hundred and twenty pound Kikuyu doorman in his neat, but hot looking gray uniform Matt remembered, was still on duty.

He opened the cab door and, as the Matt got out, said, with a large smile, "Jambo, Mr. Stark. I was happy to see your name on the incoming guest list this morning."

"Asante sana, John. You have a good memory. I'm happy to be back. Thanks for the welcome."

"You know the old Masai saying," John said with a big smile. "Big tips make for a long memory."

"John, I only gave you that big tip when I left because I didn't think I was coming back. I want a refund."

"Sorry, Bwana, it's been spent on school for my children and pombe, beer, for me."

"Well spent then," Matt said.

Matt went into the small lobby and up to the window, about the size of a small movie theater ticket booth in the States. Its size belied the efficiency and warmth of the staff.

"Good morning, Mr. Stark, welcome back. We got the message from your office about the delay. We held your small suite in the back corner of the garden as you requested."

"That's fine. Thank you."

Matt checked the information on the card that had been already filled out by the clerk. He signed it and the credit card slip and followed the porter through the open archway to the garden. As they crossed the lawn on the way to his room, Matt remembered that he was a part of the long line of Americans who had stayed there, including Theodore Roosevelt and Ernest Hemingway. Once inside he unpacked his bag, took a hot bath and lay down for a nap. From experience, Matt knew it would take him a couple of days to shake the jet lag and he wanted to be rested for his meetings at the United States Embassy tomorrow and with the Minister of Energy.

Chapter 7

The Embassy Visit

Matt had a ten o'clock appointment at the Embassy with the commercial attaché. The new embassy, built to replace the building destroyed in the 1998 bombing, was built outside town for security reasons. He arranged for a cab at nine thirty for the estimated twenty minute ride. For the first fifteen minutes of the ride, the cab struggled its way through streets jammed with old cars, new Mercedes, ubiquitous overcrowded buses and small gypsy cabs that were the main method of moving local populations in all the swarming large cities of the Third World. Kenya's special contribution, the Matatu, came in a variety of descriptions from giant buses to small minivans and all were equipped with young men hanging out the doors. Their job was to entice, and then jam in as many people as could be shoved and pushed into the vehicles to maximize the payload.

The taxi was a perfectly maintained Mercedes, probably purchased from a departing Embassy official or businessman. It reminded Matt that when he lived here, the local tribes, besides the Kikuyu and the Maasai, included those called by the locals the "Benzis." They were the wealthy local businessmen and politicians who drove the expensive German car.

The driver pulled out from the hotel onto Harry Thuku Road and took a right onto Kijabe. Matt immediately adjusted to riding on the "wrong side" of the road. They passed the Central Police station, circled a roundabout and entered Limuru Road which led into the exclusive Muthaiga area.

Trees lined the road on both sides, many loaded with blossoms. High walls surrounded the large expensive homes along the road in Muthaiga. Unarmed guards stood at their gates to protect their occupants, ambassadors, heads of foreign companies and wealthy Kenyans. The area was also the site of the famed Muthaiga Club, made familiar to the world by the movie "Out of Africa."

Six kilometers down Thika road sat the Kenyan Brewery, whose beer was one of the better legacies of the British, then a sight new to Matt appeared, a ten-foot-high concrete fence, painted white and topped with some serious looking razor wire. The fence continued for about 600 meters. The driver turned in and was confronted by concrete barriers in the road. Twenty meters beyond the barriers Matt saw a solidly built guard station flanked by a personnel carrier type vehicle.

"Sorry, sir," the driver said. "This is as far as I can take you. You've got to walk to the guard station." Matt paid the driver, thanked him and got out.

"Matt Stark here to meet the commercial attaché," Matt said, as he slid his passport to the Marine guard through the drawer in the protective glass.

"One moment, sir," said the young, but very

professional Marine. He checked a list on clipboard before him, then picked up the phone. After a quick conversation he asked Matt to enter a door to the left of the guard's window.

Matt found himself in a cell with another Marine who examined his briefcase thoroughly. The guard passed a hand held sensor over Matt's body and conducted a pat down search. Finally satisfied, he let Matt out the door in back where he gave Matt an ID card marked "Visitor" to hang around his neck.

"This will only allow you on the first floor with an escort," the guard explained. "Don't go in any other area or explore without the escort," he said emphatically.

"Can I have my passport?"

"Sorry, sir, we'll keep it until you exit."

Matt shrugged and followed the guard until they entered the embassy building. Inside the door he was met by a well-dressed, middle-aged woman with attractively graying hair.

"Mr. Stark?"

"Right."

"I'm Mary Olaf, Ms. Cohen's assistant. She's expecting you. Please follow me."

Matt trailed the woman down the hall and into and through a small outer office. As they entered the office she said, "Ms. Cohen, your ten o'clock appointment is here."

The attaché turned from the file cabinet. "Have a seat Mr. Stark." She motioned to a chair opposite her desk.

"Thanks, Mary," Matt said to the assistant. He had dealt with a number of commercial attaches over the years but none quite as attractive as the one greeting him. Melanie, about five-feet-seven-inches tall, had a slim build and straight black hair cut short. She appeared to be in her early forties. She was dressed in a dark blue business suit set off by a maroon blouse. Her handshake was firm as she welcomed Matt before she sat behind her desk.

"What can I do for you, Mr. Stark?"

"Hopefully, nothing," said Matt, "but it's always been my practice when working in a foreign country to touch base with the embassy. Just in case."

"A good practice. I wish more American business people did that. It's a little disconcerting sometimes to first meet a US businessman when something has gone wrong with his deal or he is in some other trouble and wants help."

Melanie picked up a yellow folder from her desk and extracted a letter. "I've read the letter you faxed us about your interest in getting a concession for drilling in the Chalbi Desert. I thought you had been there and done that."

"We explored the area but didn't condemn it as an oil play. It's too big an area to write off after only five wells."

Matt orally reviewed the exploration history of the area for Ms. Cohen. "My principals in Houston would like to look again. I'll try to reach some agreement with the government that will allow us to have a look around. I've got an appointment with the minister of energy tomorrow. I'll let you know if anything develops."

"Fine. You've been here before and know the

players. Fact is, I understand you know the energy minister."

"Only in a business sense. I sat across from him at a few meetings and at the signing ceremony for our concession, but most of my face to face negotiations were with the National Oil Company people."

"The minister is an interesting guy. Let me know if I can help. Every once in a while we can put in a good word if things get stuck. Usually we stay out of private business matters, but as you're dealing with the government we'd like to unofficially track your experience."

"Okay, I'll keep in touch."

"Where are you staying?"

"At the Norfolk. It was our negotiation headquarters when we were setting up here last time. It's quiet. I like it."

"Yes, a little more charm than the Hilton or the Sheraton. The garden and the birds at the Norfolk remind you you're in Africa."

"No question."

"By the way, there's a going away party at the Norfolk tonight for a representative of one of the British companies. I attend some of them to keep contact with the expatriate business community and the Kenyan businessmen. A more pleasant part of my job. Why don't you drop in? I can introduce you. Maybe you can renew some old friendships. These things are really open houses. You'll be welcome. It starts at six and should be over by eight. I'll drop in about seven. It'll be better than just sitting in your room, unless you've some other plans."

"No, I was just going to eat at the hotel, then go over my notes for my meeting with the minister tomorrow. I'll drop in for a drink and see if anyone I know is still around. Thanks for mentioning it."

"Before you go, our security officer wants to meet you. I guess he's concerned about you roaming around the desert. Do you have time?"

"Sure."

"Okay, come along. I'm a qualified escort and his office is on the first floor so your security pass is fine. By the way his name, are you ready, is Bull Durham."

After a short walk down the hall Melanie knocked at a door that had no name on it but was clearly marked, "SECURITY NO ADMITTANCE."

"Come in," answered a deep voice. Melanie and Matt entered. Bull's appearance lived up to his name. He was short, stocky, thick-necked and sported a crew cut. While he wore a white civilian shirt and red patterned tie, his whole being said military. This was emphasized by the World War I Mauser with a well polished wooden handle lying on his desk and the multitudinous certificates and pictures around the walls. Clearly, from the certificates on the wall, Bull Durham had retired from the Marines and had been all over the world.

Ms. Cohen introduced them.

"Before you think too hard about my name I want to tell you that in my youth almost everyone named Durham was called Bull. On top of that, the name I was baptized with was Percival Llywelyn, after a great grandfather. It's better than Sue, but not a whole lot. He didn't even leave us a lot of money. Anyway, when people started calling me Bull I kept the name. It saved a lot of fights, especially in the part of Texas where I grew up."

Matt, deciding this fellow had a reasonable sense of himself, smiled.

"Mr. Stark, I asked you to visit me for a couple of reasons. My primary responsibility is the security of the embassy and the people here. To maintain security we try to keep track of what goes on in all parts of the country, hopefully better than we've done in the past. In recent times there have been a number of deaths in the Chalbi Desert. Not a lot. All of them are ascribed by the government to bandits. Maybe so. I understand that you're going there."

"That's true."

"Maybe the deaths are caused by bandits, maybe not, but the weapons used are sophisticated military issue and that troubles me. Maybe the weapons are from the civil wars in Somalia, maybe not. We know that the fundamentalists have targeted us and that our intervention in Somalia left a lot of hatred. So I have two requests. Be careful, I don't want to ship another US citizen's body out of Kenya. The second is related to the first: if you see anything that causes you concern in the area let me know. Don't be a spy, just keep your eyes open."

"I can do that."

"That's not to say you ignore the district commissioner in Marsabit. He's a good man. But our interpretation of events might be different from his. We're concerned about who may be coming over that border. We still don't know how all the particulars about the explosives and people connected with the embassy bombing, you know, how they got in and out of the country."

"I appreciate the concern."

"Fine, but don't do anything. Just tell us what you see. Call me when you get back. We'll talk." He handed Matt his business card. "Sometimes we can ask a few questions that will jog your memory or bring up something that means something to us and doesn't mean anything to you. That's all I've got. Thanks for stopping by."

"Before I go, could one of you do me a favor?"

"You can ask," Bull said.

"On my way here I stopped in Vienna. The Austrian police questioned me about a man I'd met at a business meeting. He was shot and killed after our meeting. I didn't know anything and the police let me go. The Austrian policeman who questioned me was accompanied by a man who said he was Sean Casey from the US Embassy. He gave me a card. I tried to call him, but they said he wasn't there. Do you think that you can find out where I can reach him? I'd like to find out what happened."

"That sounds unusual. Let me call a friend of mine in Vienna and make an unofficial inquiry. I'll let you know what I find out."

"Thanks. Are you going to the reception tonight? Ms. Cohen has invited me."

"No. Security types don't usually go to those things. Besides, it's poker night at the Marine House. I have to go and keep those kids in line and take some of their money. If I hear anything today I'll tell Melanie. She can pass it on to you."

Melanie escorted Matt to the front door. She turned him over to the Marine guard who reversed the entry march. At the guard house Matt exchanged his visitor's pass for his passport and waited while the guard called a taxi. It took twenty minutes for the cab to arrive outside the embassy as no vehicles were allowed to park in close proximity to the wall around the compound.

Back at the Norfolk Hotel he went to his suite to read and think about what Bull Durham had told him about the desert. Security hadn't been interested in the desert when he was here before, but the embassy hadn't been blown up either.

Matt put down his briefcase and went into the bedroom to get his espionage story he'd left on the small table by the bed. He couldn't find the book. A short search found it under the bed. Must have fallen when the room was cleaned, he mused. Then he recalled the cleaners had come in before he left.

He went to the dresser to get out a clean shirt for the evening. The neat stack of shirts seemed askew. He looked around the rest of the suite. Everything seemed in place. "I'd better relax. The killing in Vienna, missing embassy guy and my spy novels have me paranoid." He shook his head and stripped to his shorts for a read and a nap.

Chapter 8

The Norfolk Hotel Reception

The paperback Matt tried to read didn't engage his mind and he soon dozed off. He woke up about six and decided to go to the reception rather than eat alone. He certainly wouldn't mind talking to Melanie some more. He shaved, showered off the day's grime and put on a light blue sport coat, white trousers and red tie. "Probably the last time I'll dress up for a while," he thought.

At seven fifteen he walked back through the garden, remembering that the embassy bombing was not the first terrorist bombing in Nairobi. On New Year's Eve, 1980 the Norfolk had been bombed, killing fifteen people and injuring eighty-five. The terrorists were never caught. Apparently they had checked into a room over the ballroom, set the timer on the bomb, took a cab to the airport and left on an international flight before midnight. No one claimed responsibility for the bombing but the Kenyan police, aided by special investigators from Scotland Yard, speculated that it was in retaliation for the Israeli raid on Entebbe, Uganda, to free hostages held by skyjackers. While Kenya and the Blocks, who owned the hotel, had no connection with the raid, the Blocks were

Jewish and that would be enough of a connection for some people.

Matt passed the bird enclosure, entered the lobby and took a right into a ballroom packed with those who knew a free party when they heard about one. He took a glass of white wine from the waiter at the door and stood to one side to observe the scene. In the middle of the room a mammoth ice sculpture sat on a table surrounded by hors d'oeuvre. Carvers stood in the four corners of the room as if guarding large cuts of beef and mutton. Between the carving stations were four full bars manned by three or four bartenders each. In addition waiters in crisp white jackets, white shirts, red ties and black pants moved through the crowd with trays of wine and champagne. Anyone who went home sober tonight wasn't trying, Matt observed.

The occasion was actually quite modest. The managing director of a small British trading company was going home to London. He was here to say goodbye and introduce his replacement. These parties, while not attended by the highest level diplomats or business people, were a regular part of social life and helped grease the wheels of commerce. They were very much appreciated by the middle management of both the government bureaus and private companies. It was also a chance for the expatriate community to visit with local business and government officials.

Matt saw a number of faces that looked familiar, but at his age more and more people looked like someone he had known only to prove to be a stranger. Finally, he did see someone he knew. Melanie wore a striking dark green cocktail dress which highlighted her green eyes, fair skin, freckles across her nose and an appealing figure. He felt a ripple of attraction, the first he could recall feeling in some time.

"Well, Matt, see anyone you know?" Melanie asked when he approached.

"Some vaguely familiar faces. I'd like to walk around 'cause I think I did see an old friend. But I want to talk to you, too."

"I still have some duty conversations, Matt. When I'm done I'll come back here. If you're not here, I'll wait a ladylike few minutes then I'm off to dreamland."

"I'll be back," said Matt. He exchanged his wine glass for a scotch to ward off the persistent offers of drinks from the waiters and circled the room again. Finally, he spotted the person he was looking for, a handsome Asian, about six feet tall, whose brilliant black hair set off smooth, tan skin. His well cut light brown business suit showed off an athletic figure. His companion was an equally attractive Asian woman with the same golden skin and black hair. Her hair hung in a long braid down the middle of her back to her waist.

The man spotted Matt before he got to them. "Matt? Matt Stark? If that's you, it's been a long time." Jemadar Amir Singh, Jay to his friends, held out his hand.

"I thought that was you, Jay. You're right, has been a while. Are you still playing tennis at Parklands?"

"Of course, but what are you are doing back here? Wait, first I would like you to meet my fiancé, Dr. Victoria DeSilva. Victoria, this is my friend and former tennis partner and opponent, Matt Stark. He's a fine fellow but has a weak serve and a poor backhand."

"I'm pleased to meet you, Matt. I think I've seen some tennis trophies with your name on them at Jemadar's."

"Yes, I let him keep them when I left because he never won any on his own," Matt chuckled, then turned to Jay. "You're engaged? I thought that you were too old to change your ways."

"Hey, I'm only forty-eight, a respected age in my culture. The prime of life. More importantly, I was fortunate to meet Victoria when she came here to work at the Aga Khan hospital. She's shown me the error of my lifestyle. Her youth, beauty and intelligence have captured my heart and soul."

"Matt," Victoria said, suppressing a smile, "while all that Jemadar says is true the fact is that I find him a suitable prospect for rehabilitation. I've accepted his proposal for strictly scientific reasons. It's an extension of some experiments I did in medical school in England trying to prove that you can teach an old dog new tricks."

"See Matt, a quick tongue to match her quick mind. But what are you doing here? How long are you staying? Have time for some tennis?"

"Whoa, one at a time. First, congratulations to you both. Secondly, I'm working on another oil deal. I can't play tennis now because I'm off to the desert tomorrow."

"Call me when you get back. We can play and have dinner. You and Victoria can get acquainted. How's the family?'

"The kids are fine but Carol died from cancer a year ago."

"My God!" Jay gasped. "That's terrible. Sorry, Matt."

"Thanks."

"How you doing?"

"Fine as long as I keep busy. Back home I was pretty lethargic."

"We'll try to help. But be careful in the desert. Kenya's not as safe as it was. Even up in the desert things have gotten worse. The civil wars of our northern neighbors have spilled over to us."

"So I've been told. How's the banking business?"

"We're doing well. Not as good as ten years ago. Low coffee and tea prices and the slowdown in the tourist business have cut our income a lot. But we make a living. No plans of leaving like some."

"Glad to hear that. It's great to see you but I've got a lady waiting. If I'm not there shortly she'll leave. We'll get together when I get back."

"Definitely."

"Pleasure meeting you, Victoria." He grinned. "Good luck on your project."

"Thanks, Matt," she said, returning the smile.

Matt took a few steps when he felt a hand on his arm. He turned. It was Jay. "I didn't want to say anything in front of Victoria but a while back I heard a strange story about the mission where you're headed. A representative of the Vatican bank was here a couple years ago and some of the local bankers had a small dinner for him. He got all liquored up and was saying something about riches in the desert. Between the booze and his accent I couldn't make out much but he wasn't talking about oil. I tried to get a hold of him the next day but he was gone. Give me a call in the morning if you can."

"Okay, sure."

Matt spotted Melanie talking to an older couple and worked his way over to her. "Matt, this is Major and Mrs. Smith-Whatley. The major is my alter ego at the British embassy. We've been comparing notes." After a short exchange of pleasantries the Smith-Whatleys excused themselves. When they were gone Melanie whispered, "It burns his crumpet that a slip of a girl holds the same rank he does. Other than that he's a nice, but stodgy, chap. His wife is a different story."

"You have interesting friends."

"Kenya attracts interesting people. Let's get out of here before the 'Goodbye, sorry to leave, Hello, happy to be here' speeches start. The bar in the Ibis Grill is quiet."

"Capital idea," Matt said, making a poor attempt to mimic Smith-Whatley's accent.

The small bar, set above and to one side of the Ibis Grill, served more as a waiting area for the grill than a public bar. Despite the name Grill, the hotel's restaurant was a fine dining room presided over by an Irish Chef with Cordon Bleu credentials. Most of tonight's guest were well into their dinners so the bar was empty. Matt and Melanie went to the last table against the wall. Melanie ordered a white wine and Matt an Irish whisky.

The drinks came and they toasted to each others' health.

"Matt, Bull got a complete negative on any Sean Casey with the embassy in Vienna."

"Weird. Well, I guess I'll catch up with him

someplace."

"No, it's stranger than that. If there were a Sean Casey there, ever, our security people would know. Bull could have found out through the back channels, if not officially."

"Back channels?"

"Yeah, the unofficial, old boy network."

"Didn't the embassy contact the police?"

"They said they did. The Austrian policeman whose name you gave us said the man with him was his Austrian partner."

"Nonsense. What about the guy outside at the airport security desk?"

"Matt, we can't investigate a host country's police. We have to take their information at face value."

"Spooky. What's going on?"

"I don't know, Matt. Let me try the old girl network. It's not as big but sometimes more reliable. I'll let you know if I find out anything. In the meantime, let's enjoy our drinks."

Matt and Melanie sipped from their glasses.

"Other than the mystery, how do you like the Foreign Service?"

"Fine, but I've been at it fifteen years and the novelty has worn off. Don't think I want to stay around for full retirement. I'm not going to be an ambassador so I've just about decided to hang it up."

"What'll you do?"

"I saw you talking to Jay. For a while I was hoping he'd sweep me up to a life of luxury, but he never called. Guess a nice Jewish girl couldn't make it in the local

Asian community." She paused then smiled at Matt's stunned expression. "Just kidding."

He laughed. "Had me going for a minute. Interesting how they refer to people from the Indian subcontinent as Asians."

"Goes back to when the British brought in the Indians to build the railroad to Uganda. Anyway I guess I'll go to Washington and try to get a job with one of the think tanks, if it won't violate some conflict of interest law."

"You're not married?"

"No ring, no husband."

"Ever been?"

"No. Close a few times."

"Prospects?"

"No. The field's pretty slim for a forty plus career girl if I can call myself that."

"I doubt that."

"What? That I can use the term 'girl'?"

"No. That pickings are slim for someone as attractive as you."

"Don't. The good ones are all taken. The rest are pretty flawed and I don't want to redo them. Or else they're looking for someone younger."

"You are young."

Melanie laughed. "Only to you, Matt. Sorry, no offense," she added suddenly.

"None taken."

"Was that a come on?"

"No, just an observation."

"Besides, you're married."

"I was. My wife died last year."

"I'm sorry, Matt."

"Don't apologize. You didn't know. I'm trying to adjust to reality."

"Got a girlfriend?"

The waiter interrupted to ask if they wanted another drink. Melanie declined but Matt ordered another.

"Just my daughter. However I've received more than my share of casseroles from the neighborhood widows. "How about you? Any boyfriends?"

"As I said, the pickings are slim. I've a pretty busy social life but no romances. The diplomatic community is very small and very talkative. Too much talk gets you sent home. I want to go home when I'm ready. I'm surprised you don't have a girlfriend."

"Melanie, I think our generation gap is showing. Your generation is blunter than we are. Why are you surprised?"

"Sorry, Matt. Guess I was more direct than I should have been. But you seem hale and hearty, and well to do on top of it. I just think you shouldn't check out on life so soon."

"I haven't and don't intend to."

"In the Jewish religion we have an observance called the Kaddish. It calls for ritual prayers for a departed loved one for eleven months after the death. But the point is that after a year the mourning is basically over. You ought to follow that. You've a lot to offer someone. Life is too short to put it on hold. I suspect your wife would like you to do it too."

"You're quite an advice giver, and on such short

acquaintance," Matt said, not unkindly.

"Sorry, my unused maternal instinct or the wine, or both."

"Appreciate the interest."

"You seem to be a genuinely nice person, and believe me, a forty plus woman who is not pig-ugly has seen too many of the other type. I just felt moved to give some advice. Besides we'll probably not see each other again."

"Don't know about that. Maybe we could have dinner when I get back."

"I'd like that."

Matt called for the check. As he rose, his leg hit the table spilling a glass of water in Melanie's direction.

"Sorry." Clumsily he tried stop the spill.

"All right, it missed me," Melanie said.

A little too stiffly, Matt escorted her to the front door. At the curb, the night doorman signaled one of the cabs waiting in line up the street.

As he helped her into the cab Matt leaned to kiss her cheek. His foot slipped off the curb and he lurched roughly into her. "Sorry, sorry, sorry," he blurted in embarrassment. "Guess I'm still jet lagged."

"Maybe," Melanie said without conviction.

"Enjoyed visiting with you," Matt said. "I'll give you a call."

"Fine," Melanie said flatly. She gave the driver her address and sank back in the seat. Nuts, she thought, another reclamation project. I don't need it. And he seemed a pretty decent guy.

Goddamn it, Matt thought as he watched the cab pull away. I screwed that up.

Matt maneuvered carefully back through the darkened garden to his room thinking about what Melanie had said. It was true that he had no new women friends since Carol died. Talking to Melanie was nice. It was a good feeling. But he was sure she wouldn't be interested in a drunk. Did he have a drinking problem? He let himself into the suite. He gave a little grimace. Well, Carol, guess I've got to get my act together.

Chapter 9

Visit to the Minister

Matt awoke the next morning slightly hung over but with a buoyancy that had been missing from his life since Carol died. He recalled his embarrassing behavior with regret. He thought about Melanie's comments on mourning. He didn't feel depressed but he saw that he must be more socially active, including mending his fences with Melanie. It wouldn't be a blot on Carol's memory. Spending more time with Melanie would be a pleasant step toward normalcy. Matt brought the tea tray in from the porch where it had been left at seven a.m. He took a cup into the bathroom, showered and shaved. In the mirror he saw a healthy, reasonably good-looking senior man. Yes, when he got back he'd have to broaden his social circle. "I'll keep you advised, Carol."

About eight o'clock he drifted through the garden into the breakfast room. It was a quarter full. Mostly groups of two and four. Tourists or businessmen. There was one group of eight. The Norfolk didn't book large parties of twenty or thirty common to the other hotels in town.

Taking fruit from the buffet, he ordered eggs, bacon,

toast and coffee from the waiter. The local paper had nothing new. A day old "Herald Tribune" came in later in the day off the early arriving airplanes from Europe. Maybe there would be something of interest in it.

Matt used to listen to BBC from London to stay current with world news but who cared now; he'd catch up soon enough. Eating slowly, he puzzled over the things he'd heard about activities in the desert. Something unusual was happening but he didn't know what, but not enough to make him change his plans. Matt was finishing when his friend Jay appeared.

"You're up early, Jay. What's up?"

"I have more to tell you than I could last night before you see the Minister."

"You look serious."

"I am. Finish your coffee and let's take a little walk."

Intrigued by the unusual request, Matt took a last sip of coffee and followed Jay out to the street. They walked away from downtown and its crowd. "What's the problem?"

"Matt, you know currency instability sometimes makes people take extreme measures to protect their wealth. Some legal, some not. Accumulating gold is one of them."

"Yeah, like the current fuss about the Russians. Going on since the beginning of time. So what?"

"Bankers hear things. Some fact, some rumors."

"Yes."

"I hear that gold's available for sale in Nairobi."

"That's pretty strange. Kenya doesn't mine gold."

"Right, and no one would smuggle it in to sell it

when they could just hold it outside the country," Jay said.

Matt considered. "So it must already be here. If it is, it would be worth a premium over world prices. Are you involved?"

"Never. Whenever anyone floats anything like this by us we cut it off quick. We don't need to give the government any excuse to take us over."

"So what has this got to do with me?"

"I don't know. This is a stretch but after last night I put together the Vatican Banker and the Kenyan gold from no place. Be careful when you go north. Something strange is going on."

"Well, thanks for thinking of me, but I don't see any connection. Do you know something you're not telling me?"

"No. But listen carefully to what the Minister says. He has an unsavory reputation."

"What's new? Why the warning?"

"A feeling, excess of caution, I don't know."

"Thanks. Got to head back."

Reversing their walk, the two men made their way through streets rapidly filling with Kenyans who worked in the city center. Jay continued past the hotel toward his office. Matt went in, put on a tie and jacket and at a quarter to ten was in front of the hotel. The doorman, John, signaled a taxi from the waiting queue. The minister's office was in walking distance but Matt didn't want to work up a sweat before the meeting nor did he want to be late. By ten, the weather, while not hot, was warming. He'd walk back. Matt's taxi pushed its nose through the swarm of people on the sidewalk waiting to enter the Utalii Building and stopped in the covered circular drive in front of the multistoried tower, the home to numerous government offices including that of the Minister of Energy, The Honorable Nicholas Kagari.

At ten minutes to ten citizens of all shapes, sizes and color were arriving to conduct business with the government. Matt paid the cab driver and walked up the short flight of stairs into a lobby. At least twenty people were waiting for each of the eight elevators. Matt worked his way into one and pushed the button for the twelfth floor. The crowd was made up of a blend of business types in their dark suits and ties, workers clutching files as if someone might steal them, modestly dressed people from the villages and an occasional tribesman in native dress, usually a Masai whose homeland was near the capital. The jam reminded Matt to ask the minister for access to the private elevator in the rear of the building, the one functionaries used to expedite their movement between floors. It saved a lot of time.

Matt pushed out of the crowded elevator and into the densely packed hallway. Using his briefcase as a tool to open the way and with many a "pardon me," he made progress toward a large Kenyan soldier in uniform guarding the way to the inner sanctum.

"I have a meeting with the minister," he told the guard, who let him pass through the door, probably more because of his white skin rather than anything he said.

Once through the door Matt stood in familiar territory. The crowd inside was more orderly, lined up against one wall of the hall. Matt went straight ahead into a small office where the two secretaries of the minister ruled. He didn't recognize one of them but to the other he said, "Hello, Frances. I'm Matt Stark. I used to visit the old minister a few years ago."

Frances smiled. "Jambo, Mr. Stark. I saw you had an appointment. Did you bring us candy and things to bribe us to get into to see the Minister early like you used to do?" She laughed.

"Not this time."

"Don't stop. Welcome back. You are well?"

"Mzuri. I'm happy to be back. Where's Mary?"

"She went back to Kitale to raise her sons and maybe have more children. The last I heard she is well. This is Rose, her replacement."

Matt and Rose exchanged greetings.

"How's your family, Frances?"

"Very well. Simon is still working at the Central Bank and Johnstone has one year left of school. He's sitting for college exams soon."

"Wish him success for me."

"I will, Mr. Stark. Things here are just the same as always, even though we have a new Minister. As usual, there is a delay. The minister was called suddenly to the State House to meet with the president. I don't know when he'll be back. He'd like you to wait."

"I'll do that. I've lots of practice."

"Come with me."

Frances led Matt down the hall to a small waiting room. It contained three chairs along each of the four walls and a low coffee table in the middle. Eight of the seats were occupied by business-suited Kenyan businessmen. Apparently the minister was as busy as ever dispensing favors and contracts. Each man had his briefcase. Six read the newspaper or papers from their files. Two worked on their laptops. Well, that's something new, Matt thought.

He uttered a general greeting which two of the sitters acknowledged. Frances announced to the group that the minister was still gone and that she'd call them when he returned, then she left.

Far from plush, the waiting room at least was a place to sit and, if you desired, do some work. Those waiting in the hallway had to stand until the minister could see them and see them he would. Most of those waiting outside were from the minister's tribe and home area. Before you could be appointed a minister in the government, you had to be elected to Parliament. While not many of the seats were closely contested you could not ignore your constituents. Taking matters to the minister for resolution was a tradition directly descended from the practice of taking matters to tribal chiefs and village elders.

As an experienced international negotiator, Matt had in his briefcase, in addition to his work papers, two paperbacks. One, the "no brainer" mystery thriller he had been reading and the other a little more serious work about the US Civil War. A course on reading material for the international business traveler should be required in MBA school, Matt thought with amusement. He usually read works about the country he was visiting when he traveled, but he had read most of the good books about Kenya when he lived here.

After more than an hour, the door opened. Frances

told the group that the minister was still with the president, then she turned to Stark. "The permanent secretary would like to see you. Follow me."

Frances led Matt to an office directly across from the minister's. As he entered Matt was pleasantly surprised to see his old friend Wilson Omburu, the Permanent Secretary of the Ministry of Energy, rise from the desk at the end of the room and hurry toward him.

"Welcome, welcome, Matt. I'm supposed to sit in your meeting with the minister. I noticed how long you were waiting and thought we could exchange a few words while you waited."

"Fine. It's good to see you. I didn't know that you were still here. I should have done my homework better."

"Hakuna Matata, Matt. You know how our government goes. Like the Brits, Ministers come and go but Permanent Secretaries stay on and on. We are the only ones who know how things work. We also manage to have a few secrets," he chuckled.

Wilson Omburu was a charming, intelligent man whose sense of humor allowed him to keep his balance through all the crises he faced as a high government official. His interest, talent and efficiency were some of the reasons Matt had been able to make progress in his struggles with the various ministries in his first negotiations in Kenya.

"Matt, it looks like you are back for a second bite of the apple. I've read your proposal. There's nothing new in it, except less work obligation and less money to be spent."

"Frankly, Wilson, that's about it. The area's been

explored and abandoned once so it shouldn't require a big exploration program. Besides, my group doesn't have the deep pockets of the major oil companies."

"Save the sales talk, Matt. Off the record, my view is that since there's no other interest we'll probably accept your deal. After a few sweeteners, of course. The final decision's up to the minister."

"Understood."

Frances opened the door. "The minister is here but must go back to the State House in an hour. He can see you for two minutes. Come along."

"I'm jumping the queue."

"That's one reason I brought you in here," Wilson said. "Let's go, unless you want to spend all day in the waiting room."

Matt followed Wilson across the hall and into an office similar to Wilson's but much better appointed. For one thing, it had a larger picture of the president surrounded by pictures of the minister with the president and other government officials at a myriad of government functions. Other awards and pictures covered the four walls. The large mahogany desk was also covered with memorabilia.

This was Matt's first sighting of Minister Kagari, a man of average height, with short hair. He was dressed in an expensive Saville Row gray suit, probably fitted on an official visit to London. The minister shot across the room, his frame exuding energy. He extended his hand in greeting but there was no smile on his face.

"Mr. Minister, I would like to present Matt Stark. Mr. Stark previously worked and lived in Kenya. He's a friend of Kenya."

"I read the brief of your proposal in the car coming to work this morning. Sit down, Mr. Stark," the Minister directed, still not smiling. "My time is limited. I've no problem with your spending money in Kenya but I'm not sure I like the economics of your proposal. Try to improve them before you talk to the National Oil Company. After you make your deal with them I'll review it and tell you what I need changed."

"You mean I negotiate a deal with them and you get to change it?"

"Very perceptive, Mr. Stark. I understand that you want to go look at the North Horr area. Go ahead. I'll tell District Commissioner Kamala to cooperate with you. Work out the details with Mr. Omburu. Good-bye. Omburu, tell Frances to send in the next person."

The minister started back to his desk. He stopped and turned again to Matt. "Your permission at this time is only to look around with regard to oil exploration. If you see or find anything else report it to the commissioner and otherwise leave it alone." He returned to his desk.

Feeling terminally dismissed, Matt followed Wilson back to his office. "And I thought the previous minister was curt," Matt said.

"That's his personality. Besides you saw all those people waiting outside who want some of his time. This is a hands-on government. Don't worry, Matt. You've got what you want for now, his okay."

"What's with the warning?"

"With all the unrest in our neighbors to the north there's an increase in theft and killing. A lot more than the government talks about. Everyone's on edge. No one wants full scale fighting. I guess he doesn't want you shot either."

"I'm not sure he cares."

"Relax. If you've any problems call me. If we sign a deal and find anything worthwhile, the minister will be as smiling and affable as any US politician running for office."

"Thanks, Wilson. I'm leaving for Marsabit tomorrow. It's good to see you. Thanks for your support." The men shook hands.

After a goodbye to Frances, Matt edged his way through the crowd in the hall and fought his way onto the elevator.

"Damn, I forgot to take the back elevator," he thought as he was jammed in. He decided to walk back to the Norfolk.

As Matt sauntered down crowded Loita Street toward University Way that bordered Nairobi University, he reflected on the meeting. That guy was abrupt even for a minister. He wants me to go away. Why?

଄ ଄ ଄

No sooner had Matt left the minister's office than the official pushed his intercom button.

"Francis, get Wellington in here now. Hold the next visitor."

Wellington Kimathi, from the minister's tribe, could have been his double except that his suit was tailored locally. Wellington was the minister's chief of security and general bag man. He arrived and stood in front of the visibly irritated minister.

"Damn it. How did Stark get his proposal approved? You know that we agreed with the Austrians to keep that area closed."

"Our man at the National Oil Company was on vacation when the request came in. Once it was approved and the American embassy knew about it we thought it would be better to let it go forward."

"Stupid. Watch him. I don't want him screwing up my deal."

"I will."

"Hear anything from the Austrians?"

"They met him in Vienna. They don't think he knows anything but they're following him."

"What a circus. They're a bunch of fanatics. I don't want any more of their thuggery around here. And I don't want anything to happen to Stark unless he knows something. No sense in drawing attention. If nothing else it will get the Americans poking around. What a bother for a relative pittance. Don't screw up again. Out."

ଓ   ଓ   ଓ

Matt stopped to stare at a large white building, the local hotel of the Mount Kenya Safari Club. It was ornate but without the natural beauty and animals of the original club at the foot of Mount Kenya. The Norfolk is much more fun, he thought, as he waited to cross the street. Suddenly he felt a jostle and slid off the curb into the traffic. The oncoming vehicle swerved and glanced off

Matt's brief case that he had instinctively stuck out to protect himself. Knocked to the ground, he lay dazed. Finally focusing, he looked up into a number of concerned black faces. Convincing them that he wasn't injured, he accepted their help in getting up. The driver had stopped his car and was most apologetic.

"Sorry, sorry sir but you came out suddenly. I could not stop. You must have slipped."

"Yes. Okay. No harm done," Matt stammered. Shaken but not otherwise injured, he finally persuaded the driver that he was all right. Gathering himself together, he extricated himself from the solicitous crowd and went on his way.

Safely across the street, Matt wondered if he had just imagined the jostle. It definitely was not a hard push. I need to sit in front of the Norfolk, have a cold Tusker and a sandwich, relax and smirk at the tourists, he thought. He put his briefcase in his room, changed out of his suit, and did exactly that.

Chapter 10

Chalbi Desert Drive

Matt's drinks after his meeting with Kamala extended to a few. He woke with a headache, showered, dressed and went to meet Moses. The men had a traditional English breakfast of eggs, rashers, blood sausage and tomato followed by some untraditional and delicious Kenyan coffee in the lodge dinning room. It had taken a little persuasion to get the food served early enough so that they could be off at dawn.

Matt paid the bill while Moses went out for a final check with the driver, Daniel, in the car park of the lodge. Matt had called the nun's room twice the previous evening with no response. Finally, he'd left a message that they'd leave at dawn and he'd arranged for an early breakfast. Now when she didn't appear at breakfast he felt concerned, but what did he know of nun's habits. He groaned at his pun.

Matt called the nun's room once more. As he held the desk phone, a woman came into the lobby. She wore a long khaki skirt and a simple white blouse with a wooden cross on a plain silver chain around her neck. Otherwise she looked like someone out of an Aer Lingus "Visit

Ireland" poster.

Her ivory skin was highlighted by red cheeks and short auburn hair. Her green eyes sparkled. Although she was about five-foot-six inches in height, she appeared shorter because of the pounds on her frame. She carried a jacket, hat and small bag. She walked up to Matt, who set the receiver back into the cradle.

"Sorry I missed you, Mr. Stark. I went on a game drive last evening with one of the guides and the time got away from us. This morning I had my breakfast in my room while I packed a few things and said my prayers. I assure you that I am not antisocial."

Matt shook her hand. "I'm sure you're not."

"I like to get out into the green and see the water when I can. It's a nice change from the desert. The green reminds me of home."

"See anything interesting?"

"Oh, my yes. The usual elephants and kudus and the like, but I especially love the birds. They're brilliant."

"Glad you had a pleasant drive. Our vehicles are outside and loaded."

"I'm ready."

Matt turned and thanked the manager. "We could be back in a few days."

"No problem, Sir. We'll have room for you. Be careful.

"We will," Matt assured him.

Matt, dressed in his desert attire of khaki pants, shirt and jacket, completed by the most important item, a khaki hat, looked like the American tourists who poured into Kenya with lots of bucks wearing clothes purchased from

Abercrombie and Fitch. They went to the plush bush camps on escorted tours where they could have worn dinner clothes. The camp drivers and workers were sharply dressed as well because most of the tourists left their bush clothes behind at the camp; easier than hauling them home, storing them in the suburbs for a few years and then giving them to Goodwill.

Moses, a smart local, wore a pair of light brown slacks, a white shirt with long sleeves and a wide brimmed hat for protection against the sun. Daniel was dressed like Matt, but that was required by the company he worked for in Nairobi. The tourists expected it, and it looked neat.

"All set, Daniel?" Matt asked.

"Ndiyo, Bwana." Once used to show a master servant relationship, the term Bwana was now the same as Sir or Mister and was used freely in conversation as society had evolved.

"Sister, why don't you join Moses and me? The two guards can follow us in the other Rover. That's more sociable and just as safe."

"You're right," she said.

Matt made the arrangements with the guards. Sister Columba and Moses settled themselves, in the back and front seats of the vehicle, respectively. Before getting in himself, Matt asked the key question, "Does the air conditioner work, Daniel?"

Daniel smiled. "Yes, sir, wouldn't want the explorer to get too hot."

Matt laughed. "I'm no Lawrence of Arabia and neither are you. Be careful or you'll be assigned one of the non-air conditioned vehicles. You'll have to take out tourists in it until you retire."

"Not to be desired, Bwana."

"Let's start this safari."

They drove slowly through the trees and down the mountain. The air was still clear and cool and they could hear some of the early rising birds calling to each other. No other animals could be seen. Apparently still slowly waking from their sleep, they remained deep in the forest. After a little less than twenty-six kilometers, they emerged onto the flat surface of mud and salt that was the Chalbi desert. It extended about two hundred kilometers from Marsabit to Lake Turkana. No road went directly from one point to the other. Instead the route went northwest to North Horr then southwest another sixty or seventy kilometers to the lake. The first portion of the route was a combination of trail, road and track, none of it paved, following an old trade route. Matt's group had to navigate it northwest for the ninety-two bumpy miles to the village of North Horr, population unknown, except that there are many more goats than people.

"I was surprised the first time I arrived in the desert," Sister Columba said. "I thought there would be lots of sand, but there isn't any. I learned that what makes a terrain a desert is no water and no vegetation. The sand is extra."

"Most of the deserts on earth are like the Chalbi. The sandy ones have better press agents and look better in the movies," Matt said.

The Range Rover moved slowly, jerking along the road, jarring spines as it went.

"How did you and Commissioner Kamala become friends?" the nun asked.

"I worked with him when I first came here several years ago."

"You said you looked for oil a few years ago. Are you really serious about looking here again?"

"Sure, my employers think they have a new slant on things. You can always find a geologist to convince those who hold the purse strings to spend a few million in the quest for black gold. New science and interpretation of old data aside, there's always anecdotal evidence that keeps searches alive. Libya's a good example."

"Why?"

"There was no oil produced in Libya in the early fifties. The government opened up the country to foreign companies. Seventeen applied. They drilled, spent a bundle, found nothing. Most of the companies were selling off supplies and pulling out when Esso made a big strike in 1958. The rush was on. Every old oil man has stories like that."

"Seems stupid to spend millions with no new evidence."

"Maybe," Matt said. "This time the risk and the money's not as big. We won't commit to drilling any wells. All we want is what we call a seismic option, a license to look around. We may spend a million or so. If seismic shows anything promising, we have the right to drill some wells and extend the agreement. Plus we have access to prior work done by other companies on file with the national oil company."

"A million or so? How about giving some of that to

our mission?"

"Unfortunately it doesn't work that way."

"I know, but it's still too bad."

Matt smiled and deliberately changed the subject. "How did you end up out here, Sister?

"Pretty simple. I was a nurse and joined the Missionary Sisters of Our Lady in Dublin when I decided I needed a little more depth in my life. They sent me here. This is what missionary sisters do."

"That sounds too simple. There must be more."

"No. Whatever I did or was before is behind me. As they say. What you see is what you get. Sorry it's not more exotic."

"I didn't mean to pry. Sorry."

"Don't worry, most nuns have pretty simple backgrounds. We're just women with a different job and lifestyle. I see a tape deck. Any music?"

"Moses, what have we got?"

Moses looked through the collection of tapes in a satchel. "Do you like Irish music, Sister?" Moses asked.

"It depends, I like the Dubliners. I do favor traditional music, but most anything will do."

"Here we go," Moses said. "Strauss's New Year's concert by the Orchestra der Wiener Volksperl of Vienna. Just the thing to listen to on drive through the desert." He smiled.

"Weird choice. Put it in but low."

As the waltz started, Matt said, "Maybe it'll keep our minds off the heat."

"It's okay in here but it'll get to the high nineties outside. It reflects off the dried ground," Moses observed.

"It's worse when a little rain falls, because it's still hot and the ground gets sticky and impassable," Daniel said.

"As our Arab friends say, 'Allah puts oil where he wants to. It is one of His ways of playing jokes on us.'" Moses laughed.

"Unfortunately, we're geologically a little late in our search. A couple of hundred thousand years ago we could have taken a dip in fresh water here and dried off in the shade of the woods," Moses said.

"Were there people around?" Columba asked.

"Sure, when I came up with a scientific team from the National Museum, we found stone tools, pottery, beads and broken bones near North Horr. Seems it was a pretty busy area at one time. Wait, this is the last number on the tape and I missed it due to the chatter. Daniel, start that over and let's enjoy this kidney-jarring ride in relative quite for a while. No offense, Matt," Moses said with a smile.

"None taken."

The three dozed as best they could as the vehicle inched along the eroded road.

After sometime, Matt said, "Daniel, your eyes are better than mine. Is that a mirage off to the north or is something moving out there?"

The question alerted the group. Kamala's warning came quickly to mind. Matt was glad for the guards trailing in the Rover.

"Get the glasses," Matt said reaching for a pair.

The vehicle stopped and three pairs of state-of-the-art binoculars pointed north.

"Relax, I think," said Moses. "It looks like a group of Gabbra tribesman on the move with their camels."

"Looks like a bunch of sailboats to me."

"Those are house poles tied to the camels. The Gabbra get their food and wealth from their animals, camels, sheep and goats mostly. They pack their goods and houses on the camels and take off. Got to keep moving to find enough vegetation," Moses said.

"Their houses?"

"Right, they're made of house poles with skins and sisal mats wrapped around to form the covering. It's broken down, household goods packed and put on a frame built on the camels back. What you see that looks like a sail boat is a bundle of the longest house poles sticking up."

"For a geologist you know a lot about this."

Moses shrugged. "There are not a lot of jobs for geologists in Kenya. I put in a couple years at the Museum in Nairobi and made a few trips up here with anthropologists from Europe."

"Anything else we should know about you, Moses?"

"All in good time."

"What about shiftas among the Gabbras?"

"Not likely. The shiftas don't disguise themselves. They just pop on you. Besides if you look again you'll see that they're not moving toward us, but parallel and to the east."

"That's a relief."

The diversion over, the passengers tried to pillow their heads for a cat-nap.

A little while later Daniel said, "Bwana, we have

gone about fifty kilometers. By my reckoning we should be fifteen kilometers from Kalacha Dida. Somewhere along here is the start of the road you bulldozed south to the well site. There are no monuments or landmarks, so I can't tell for sure."

"Let's see if we can find anything."

Matt and Moses got out. The heat slapped them in the face and perspiration quickly beaded on their foreheads. Even behind sunglasses, their eyes had difficulty focusing. Riding in the air conditioning made it seem even hotter outside. Daniel told the driver of the following vehicle that they were going to look around a little. Matt and Moses stepped off in opposite directions, carefully examining the south side of the road for any markers or sign of an old cut into the desert. Neither saw indications in the dirt or brush of a road that at one time handled thousands of tons of equipment and supplies.

They returned to the cool air of the Rover and paused to get their breaths.

"You sure you have the right spot?" Matt wiped sweat from his face and took a drink of cool water.

"It's my best guess. Look at the map. There are no check points around here so all we have to work with is distance estimates."

"The well site was six kilometers south of the road. Let's drive dead south into the desert and see if we find anything. We've got time."

"Matt, let's not wander around in the desert. It's too easy to get lost, besides, Sister Columba has to get back to the mission."

"Right. Sorry, Sister, let's go on."

"No," Sister said. "Why don't I go on with the other vehicle and a guard. You do your looking around. It may save you time later. I won't be any worse off than before with my own driver and guard."

"You sure?"

"My friend, I've lived out here for a few years and have been in more dangerous situations than this. Worry not."

"Fine, I would like to get a quick look around."

Matt put Sister's bag in the second vehicle, spoke briefly to the driver, and waved the other vehicle down the track to North Horr. He got back in the first Rover.

"Drive straight south by the compass. If we don't see anything we reverse and come straight back. No problem. Okay with you, Daniel?'

"Just a short drive is okay." Moses reluctantly agreed. Daniel headed the vehicle straight south.

After a few bumpy meters Moses said, "Lets hope we don't break an axle on this stuff."

"Hey," said Matt. "This is a Range Rover and not a Peugeot. It's supposed to go over rough ground."

Daniel maneuvered the vehicle carefully around the larger bumps and hillocks in the desert. As far as the eye could see, even when aided with binoculars, was a flat, brown landscape. When they reached the self-imposed six-kilometer limit, Daniel stopped the Rover on a small rise. Matt and Moses got out.

Careful not to touch the searing metal with his bare hands, Matt clambered onto the hood of the vehicle. He slowly scanned the horizon with his binoculars. Nothing broke the flat cratered landscape. The various shades of brown earth were occasionally punctuated by spots of white and gray that were collections of salt or other minerals. Nothing indicated the land was hospitable to life. Matt felt like he was one of Rommel's or Montgomery's tank commanders in the Libyan desert in World War II looking for their nemesis. Maybe he was.

He got back into the cool air of the vehicle and pulled out some photos. "Look," he said, showing the other two pictures of the drill site. "We built a city for over two hundred people. Living quarters, infirmary, dining hall, kitchen, landing strip and topped off by a multistory drilling rig. Not a trace. You'd think there'd at least be some evidence of the huge pit we dug for dumping the water and chemical muds we used for drilling."

"Matt, we filled that all in and it weathered over," Moses said.

"Guess we were more effective than I thought."

"Any sight of the metal water well heads we left?"

"No. Out here there really isn't anyone to use them on a regular basis so I guess nature just took over."

"Well, I hoped we could find something to help us. Let's go. Come back tomorrow and try to check out our coordinates. You know what really strikes me as odd now that we are out here in the desert?"

"What?"

"That those guys in Houston insisted that I come out to the site. It's like they expected us to find something on the ground. Guess they don't know much about deserts. Look, before we leave let's circle and look at the ground for a few hundred yards out. Might see something."

"Okay." The vehicle moved slowly in concentric, ever widening circles while the men examined the ground on either side of the vehicle.

"Wait!" Moses yelled.

"What?"

"I don't know, a glimmer off to the right."

Matt jumped out and scratched in the dirt. "Well I'll be damned. A plastic water bottle with a European label. This is recent. Somebody's been here lately. The nomads don't carry these, and it's off the path for tourists. Maybe those guys Kamala told us about. Let's look around here a little more."

A large gray boulder sat ten yards away. The south of it was shielded from the prevailing wind. The ground showed tire tracks.

"Bingo. Mark this on our map," Matt said. "We'll come back tomorrow."

"Right," Moses agreed.

Daniel turned the Rover around and followed Matt's direction dead north to the road where they had turned west. In a short time, palm and fever trees indicated a settlement.

"That's Kalacha Dida," Moses said.

Primitive thatched huts were visible among the leaves. A track for vehicles ran from the road to a spot shaded by a group of palm trees. None of the trees were over six feet tall but palm fronds sprouted out of them from the ground up. No naked tree trunks as seen on the palm trees in North Africa. Three or four women sat under a group of trees.

"Daniel, drive in there. Let's see if they've seen

anyone around here recently."

Daniel parked the Rover in some shade. "I know a few words of the local languages. Let me go visit while you stretch your legs," Moses said.

"Fine," Matt replied.

Matt watched an animated exchange between Moses and the women punctuated by a lot of waving and pointing.

Moses came back. "I'm not quite sure, but I think that the men are off with the goats and camels looking for grazing. They should be back in a couple of days. One or two of the men might have worked at the drill site and could lead us to the general area of the site. They used to get their water from a small well here, but it dried up."

"Anything else?"

"Yes, two Wazungus went through here a week or so ago. They must be the two Europeans that Kamala told us about. As near as I could understand they stopped for water. They tried to ask some questions, but since they didn't know the language, they had to use pointing and signs to communicate. They looked around, took some pictures and took off in the direction indicated by the women."

"Where was that?"

"Toward the northwest."

"Doesn't sound like our guys. Well let's get on to North Horr. It's about fifty more miles. We can come back tomorrow and hope the one who worked at the site is back. Even if he isn't, we can take a little more scientific approach with our search."

Moses went back and told the women that if the men

came back they should stay in the village. They'd be back tomorrow and pay for some help. He wasn't sure how well the communication between them worked.

The group resumed the slow, bumpy ride. After two hours, speed took second place to minimum jarring to the spine. Shortly they again saw trees and huts in the distance. It looked like Kalacha Dida, only larger. It was North Horr.

A bell tower surmounted by a cross rose above the trees. A short way from the village, the road was outlined on both sides by white stones about a yard apart from each other. They came to a "T" intersection. Instead of driving straight across the barren ground the thirty meters to the church they turned right, went a few meters, turned left and followed the marked road through an opening in a low stone wall. The stones led them to an area among the trees in back of the church where they parked. Off to the right Matt saw two elongated buildings with metal, not thatched, roofs.

The three got out of the vehicle and looked at the church with wonderment and respect. Matt had heard about the church from hands who worked the rig but had not been here himself. Like the wall, it was made of rock and cement. It rose two stories, maybe fifteen feet high. The roof slanted up to a peak about eighteen feet high. The bell tower, rising from the edge of the roof was another six or eight feet high. Two narrow windows about two feet by four feet were just below a half circle window in the back wall. Matt guessed that these were behind the altar.

As the men walked around to the front of the church

they saw two more one-story buildings with metal roofs off to one side inside the stone wall. The longest building, they later learned, contained the dispensary, or surgery, as the Irish called it, the mission offices and the guest quarters. The second building housed the nuns' living quarters, including a kitchen, dining room and a parlor/library for reading and relaxing. The third building, the first they had seen, contained the storehouse and repair shop. The third building had a lean-to attached to it.

Solid, glistening black doors, eight feet tall greeted Matt as he turned the corner. They must be mahogany from west Kenya, he thought. The wood had been cut into planks and attached side to side but Matt could see no seams. The top half of the right door was carved to show three figures that appeared to represent the Trinity. In the top half of the left door was carved a face of a woman that Matt took to be the Virgin Mary, with flowers and angels around her. The carvings were primitive, powerful and beautiful. After looking at them a short time he reached out and felt their smoothness. Opening the right door they walked into a church bursting with color.

Against a light blue background were murals in the brightest hues of blue, red, yellow, orange and violet of various events in the life of Christ. He was a black Christ and all the people in his world were black, even the Roman soldiers in the Crucifixion scene.

Matt and Moses slowly walked down the one side aisle then back up the other. The cyclorama was overwhelming. The flat ceiling was the same light blue as the walls, like the enormous African skies. At the far end of the church was a simple altar with two sets of candlesticks. The windows Matt had seen before were behind the altar and let the sun shine into the church and onto the altar. Matt resolved that he would come back to look at each mural in depth after they had settled in. Without speaking Matt and Moses each returned to their favorite mural.

Finally Matt spoke. "We have to come back and take pictures."

"That's certain. I haven't seen anything like this in Nairobi."

"Let's find our hosts."

Outside Matt started toward a building where he saw natives sitting on the steps. Just before he got there, the door opened and a white woman came and walked toward him. She was about five-feet-five inches tall, with close cut black hair and blue eyes and dressed like Sister Columba in a short-sleeved white blouse and a khaki skirt that came just below her knees. Her Celtic skin was dotted by freckles across the bridge of her nose. She appeared to be in her early forties. A small wooden cross hung from her neck on a length of black leather.

"A hundred thousand welcomes," she said extending the old Gaelic greeting in English. "I'm Sister Brendan. You met Sister Columba. That's the clinic I just came from. I thought I'd head you off and take you to your rooms for a cool drink and a lie down. Brother Sebastian will get you settled. I have to go back to work. As usual we have a full house." It was clear who set the agenda here.

"Thank you. I'm Matt Stark and this is Moses Mrabi.

Our driver, Daniel, is still with the car. We were just admiring the art in your church," Matt hurried to follow Sister Brendan's quick walk.

"Yes, very impressive," she said. "Artists from Wood Carvers Alley in Nairobi carved the doors and brought them up by truck. The paintings inside were done by volunteers from Paa ya Paa studio in Nairobi when the church was opened. Long before my time. Every year or two the head of the gallery brings some of his artists up to keep the murals fresh. They understand that they're not to tell anyone about it because we don't want this to be a tourist destination or place of pilgrimage. All we need is one 'miracle' to ruin our clinic."

"Have you had any?"

"Miracles? That's a matter of opinion and faith. Officially no. I understand from Sister Columba that you're going to look around that old drill area for a few days."

"Yes, we've already had a brief look about, but need to go back."

"Nothing but bare desert out there now but you're welcome to stay with us. This end of the building holds the guest bedrooms." She pushed opened the door of the low slung structure.

"You each have a bedroom. We have accommodations for your driver in the other building. Brother Sebastian should be right along. He'll bring some cool water. Clean up and rest then join us at seven for a wee dram before dinner. We have prayers in the church at six if you want to join us. No obligation." She laughed. "Sebastian will tell you where we eat, goodbye." She hurried out the door and to the clinic.

The men walked to the Rover and Daniel drove it to their quarters. As they were opening the back of the vehicle to unload, a short, wiry man, his skin darkened by the African sun, approached from the third building. An African accompanied him. The white man walked vigorously despite a pronounced limp.

"Welcome. I'm Brother Sebastian." He extended his hand in greeting.

Matt shook a hand, hardened by work that seemed to belong to a much larger man. Sebastian stood about five-feet-five inches in height, and much of his one hundred twenty-five pounds, appeared to be in his arms. His gray hair, what little there was of it, was combed straight back. Matt could not tell if his dark eyes were brown or black.

"This is Joshua," he continued in an English with a strong Italian accent. "We'll get you settled in your quarters and he'll show your driver where he'll be staying."

"Thanks. I'm Matt Stark and this is Moses Mrabi. Daniel is our driver."

"You had better bring everything inside," Sebastian said.

"Do you have much theft here?"

"No, not really, but the people are incredibly poor. Anything loose, they might borrow."

They soon had the Rover load distributed between the two small bedrooms. Each room contained a single bed, a small dresser for clothes, a pitcher and bowl for washing and a thermos of drinking water. Pegs were on the wall for anything that needed hanging. Decorations were a cross, a picture of the Virgin Mary, a picture of Mount Kenya and a picture of the president. A Bible, a couple of detective stories, *Rumpole at the Old Bailey*, and two books by the Irish author Brian Moore were scattered about. One electric light hung from the ceiling and another was attached to the bed headboard. Three candles and a box of matches stood ready for emergencies.

"There's a shower at the end of the hall. Let us know if you need anything else. I'll be in the workshop or in my quarters till prayers at six. Otherwise I'll see you at dinner."

"Fine," Matt said. "Thanks again. Daniel, we'll see you later and discuss our plans for tomorrow."

"Ndiyo, bwana."

Matt and Moses went to their rooms. The cool water from the pitcher felt good on Matt's face and arms. The print in the paperback became fuzzy as he began to doze off. The last thought he had before he went to sleep was to wonder what the missing diplomat in Vienna had to do with this remote place in the desert.

Chapter 11

North Horr

Matt and Moses walked to the building where the evening meal would be served. Sebastian joined them as they entered the building. Sisters Brendan and Columba were waiting inside.

"Would either of you like a drink before dinner?" Brendan asked.

"Maybe after dinner," Matt said.

Moses also declined.

"Well, let's sit down and say grace." They all bowed their heads as Sister Brendan thanked God for the food, their health and Matt and Moses's safe trip.

Rousing "Amens" ended the blessing.

Sister Brendan rang a bell on the table and two African women entered the room with serving plates.

"Welcome to the desert," Sister Brendan said. "We have no Irish salmon. Our specialty here is goat. We cook it many ways. Tonight it's roasted. Once in a while we substitute camel. Fortunately we get some things shipped up from Nairobi so we have rice and a few of the wonderful vegetables available in Nairobi to supplement the meat. We usually don't have dessert but we have very good Kenyan tea or coffee to finish off."

The serving women passed the plates; the diners helped themselves. Matt noticed that Sister Columba's portions were a little bigger than the others.

Sister Brendan monopolized the dinner conversation reciting the history of the mission, its founding just before World War II by the Vatican at the urging of the local bishop and the Vatican representative in Nairobi. Sister Brendan's order, Ladies of the Missions, from Ireland, supplied the nurse-nuns to staff it. In the beginning, religious brothers from Ireland had supported them. At the end of war the mission was fixed up and expanded by a work group sent by the Vatican. Brother Sebastian had come with the work group more than fifty years ago and stayed. The nuns were rotated by their order. Sister Brendan had been here five years and Sister Columba three.

One of the servers returned. Sister Columba took a small second helping of the meat and a little rice. The others declined further food. The conversation grew more lively as the diners exchanged their impressions of the awesome desert. They concluded that there were certainly reasons for the mystics to go off to the desert to meditate. Matt volunteered that his prior visit were fly-ins to the well site only and he had not been to North Horr. No one spoke of personal matters.

As Sister Columba finished her second helping, Sister Brendan said, "Matt, Moses, would you like some tea or coffee in the sitting room? It's a little more comfortable. We don't follow the American custom of sitting at the table after dinner."

"Thank you, but I have some reports to finish," Moses said. "Please excuse me."

Sister Columba rose too. "I've got to finish my inventory in the dispensary."

"I'll join you for tea," Matt said.

Sister Brendan led the way to two comfortable chairs opposite a sofa with a low table between them. They were solid and obviously handmade, like the dining room table and chairs. Sister disappeared into the kitchen and shortly reappeared with a tray holding a beautiful Beleek tea pot and matching cups and saucers. Matt admired their elegance.

"These are one of the few luxuries I allow myself. I brought them back from one of my trips home to Wicklow, hand carried them like eggs on the plane. They're one of the last mementos of my family. The water is always on the boil for tea, Matt. We also have some Jameson's if you'd like a wee drop."

"No, I don't want to take your supply. It must be hard to get."

"Actually, we've had this for years. We don't drink. Some visitor left it with us sometime ago."

Matt and Sister Brendan settled into their chairs. Sister poured.

"Sugar or milk, Matt?"

"Nothing thanks. Maybe a little lemon. I'm curious, what's a nice girl like you doing in a desert like this?"

"Matt," Sister said with a smile. "You need a better line than that. You've watched too many bad movies or read too many poorly written books."

"If I'm prying excuse me.

"It's really pretty simple. I grew up in an Ireland and a Church run by men. Extremely conservative men at that, or is that redundant. Women knew, or should have known their place, and it was not very far from home. In addition, I was one of nine children raised mainly by my mother. Da was not around much. He had a broad definition of a wee drop."

"That must have been difficult."

"It was, but there was enough love all around. We weren't as bad off as those people in the book *Angela's Ashes*. That was ugly. We scraped by."

"How did you get your education?"

"I was bright and my mother somehow talked my way into a convent school. Got a great education. I won a scholarship to University College, Dublin."

"What did you study?"

"I was an voracious reader so I studied English. It was a natural fit. Look around before you go and you'll see the best library north of Nairobi."

"I'll do that. In the meantime I can leave what I have. Most of the books I have are page turners for airplane reading. Not much to stretch the brain."

"Leave them if you are done. We can filter out the junk."

"We did bring some music. I'll leave it."

"Thanks. We need a little more variety."

"Well, it's still a long way to Dublin. How'd you get here?"

"You're a glutton for punishment. I'll give you the short version. Dropped out of University, did odd jobs, writing for a newspaper, enjoyed the night life of Dublin.

Spent quite a bit of time at the Brazen Head and lesser known pubs. But, as the novels would have it I was not "*happy.*" After my mother died, my father disappeared and my surviving siblings decided that we all hated each other. I thought about other things I could be doing with my life. One of the alternatives was the religious life and particularly nursing. This wasn't a quick process, but I went through it."

"Lots of us all go through internal examinations but we don't end up with such extreme results."

"This isn't extreme. Opportunities for single women in Ireland were limited. As late as the nineties the women representatives to the peace talks were greeted by mooing sounds and calls of 'cow' by the 'enlightened' Irishmen from both the North and the Republic. I guess I shouldn't have been too surprised. These were the same people who think you get peace by blowing innocent people up. Anyway, I felt becoming a nun and a nurse was a way to have an independent life."

"If the tea's still hot, I'll have some more, please."

Sister Brendan poured for Matt, then herself and sat down.

"Well, did you get what you wanted?"

"Hardly."

"What happened?'

"Are you sure you're interested?"

"Yes. I'm going through a transition myself. Knowing how other people handle change is helpful."

"I'm not sure our situations are similar, but to abbreviate things, I did my nurse's training and novitiate on parallel courses. I liked the hands-on nursing but soon found myself in administration. Then the politics got too much for me.

"Women were still second class citizens in the Church. Issues like birth control and abortion are still controlled by the Church in Ireland. I had a lot of donnybrooks with the Archbishop and my superiors. Around that time I started to read some of the writings of Bernard Haaring, the German Catholic scholar who died in 1945. He said to be a Catholic was to meet the needs of all people, not just Catholics. For those of us who had grown up thinking the obligation of our faith was to hop step through a legalistic set of rules that defined sin, his philosophy was liberating."

"You sound like a rebel."

"Not me. Just concerned and independent. Anyway, after losing too many battles with Church authorities, I heard that Sister Margaret wanted to come back to Ireland from Kenya because her parents were sick. I volunteered for the job."

"Weren't you overqualified?"

"Not in the eyes of my superiors. They thought it was a great place for me to go. They agreed in a minute. Here I am."

"Why such a remote place?"

"Like I said, to get away from the artificial dissension, discord, rules and regulations."

"I thought you followed directives from Rome."

"The Pope is there. We're here. His job is to make big pronouncements. Ours is to heal the people. If he doesn't want women to be priests and leaders in the Church that's his loss, and ours, to the extent that we can't have the Holy Mass every day. Our only rule is to help people. If I have a vocation, that's it. It's not arguing about some interpretation of the Bible or some man-made rules allegedly defining our relationship with God. Here we work with the people and talk to God as we can. Hopefully I'm still in the Church. If I'm not maybe it should change."

"Pretty strong stuff. How do Sister Columba and Brother Sebastian feel about all this?"

"After a few discussions when I first got here it soon became clear where we agreed and disagreed. We concentrate on where we agree and do our work. Good plan for the world, Matt." Brendan paused, then said, "After that lecture do you want some more tea or a drop of the Jamesons?"

"I'll try the Jamesons and then to bed."

"Ah, I've driven another man to drink." She laughed as she walked toward the kitchen. She returned with a quarter full bottle of whiskey, a small Waterford crystal glass and some ice.

"No ice for me. I admire the Waterford crystal. You've brought some of the best products of Ireland to this desert."

"Yes, too bad I couldn't bring some of its rain."

Matt poured a generous portion of whiskey, added a little water and settled back into his chair. He smelled the aroma and took a small sip of the "water of life."

"Matt, what's your wife doing while you're here?"

"She died a year ago."

"I'm sorry. You must miss her."

"Yes, I do." Matt sipped a little of his whiskey and

looked off into space. After a little pause he said, "That's what I meant when I said I was going through a transition. I haven't talked about it much until recently when I opened up about it with the wife of a friend of mine in Houston. Then I mentioned it to a woman I met in Nairobi. I guess the doctor was right, the more I face it as a reality, the better I feel." Matt then told Sister Brendan a condensed version of Carol's illness, their decision and its consequences.

"Matt, I don't hear much of a reference to God in all this."

"Well, maybe not God. We were raised Episcopalian and had been away from formal religion for some time, but there was a definite spiritual element to the last days." Matt told the nun about the visit to the church that should not have been open but was.

"I see the hand of God," she observed.

"Maybe."

Outside, the sun set and the desert air cooled on the way to a chilly night. Matt and Sister Brendan sat in silence for some time.

Finally, Matt said, "We'll drive back to try to look for the old drill site in the morning. I don't know how long we'll be gone."

"Take lots of liquids. It gets searing out there. We'll be here when you come back. May God hold you in the palm of his hands."

"Good night, Sister. Thanks for the conversation."

Matt walked toward his room and looked at a million stars in the clear desert sky. He remembered sitting with Carol outside their tent on the safaris they had taken while living in Kenya. The memory was a pleasant end to a full day. He wondered if Melanie was looking at the African skies. It was different viewing it from a big city. He walked slowly to his room. Thinking about Carol and Melanie in the same context seemed a natural thing to do.

Chapter 12

The Discovery

After breakfast, the men got out their maps and estimated the location of the drill site.

"Let's repeat our drive the six kilometers south from our marker. When we get to the approximate location, we can drive a grid pattern over the area," Moses said.

"Sounds logical to me," Matt responded.

Just before the sun rose, Daniel headed the Land Rover back toward Kalacha Dida. They found the nomads back from their safari. One of them had indeed worked on the drill site as a laborer. His English was passable, but as he had not been in the village when the recent visitors came through, he had no information.

"Has there been anyone else asking about the well?" Moses asked.

"Long ago."

"How long?"

"Past the last long rainy season."

"Over a year," Moses interpreted.

"They didn't leave the bottle. Maybe they were the ones killed last year," Matt said.

"Maybe."

Matt and Moses negotiated a fee for the nomad to accompany them into the desert. The four of them drove back along the road to the marker they had left. They drove south into the desert six kilometers then continued south to follow the grid in a primarily north/south manner to avoid looking into the sun.

Traveling slowly, less than ten miles per hour, they periodically stopped to examine anything of possible interest anyone spotted. Five hours passed before they completed the grid.

"What a waste of time," Matt said disappointed. "Nothing's out here."

"If there is, we won't find it this way," Moses added.

"All right Daniel, let's go back to the mission and drop off our guide on the way."

Back at the mission, Daniel drove Moses over to the living quarters and dropped Matt off at the storage shed where they unloaded the tools they had borrowed in the event they had found anything. Then he drove the vehicle to the service area to refuel and clean it up.

Matt picked up some of the tools and entered the shed. Wiping them off, he replaced them in their designated spots. The storage area was well organized. Sebastian had a place for everything. Then Matt noticed one thing out of place. A box in one corner of the shed apparently had fallen. As he went to place it back on the shelf he noticed something in the floor.

ଓ ଓ ଓ

"Sister Brendan, could we talk? It's important," Matt

asked when he located the nun in the main building

"Certainly, Matt."

"This package will interest you."

Matt laid a blanket wrapped package on the conference table. He undid the blanket, revealing a plastic wrapping. Inside the plastic were three pieces of metal coated with oil and three small boxes. If either Matt or Sister Brendan had been experts in firearms they would have identified them as an AK-47 assault rifle with folding metal stock, a Mini-Uzi submachine gun, fourteen inches long and a Walther PP. All compact and deadly. Matt's long ago experience in the military, office bound as it was, let him know that he was not looking at standard issue for a religious brother.

"Jesus, Mary and Joseph," Sister Brendan breathed. "Where did you find this arsenal? Whose is it? Certainly the IRA boys haven't been around here."

"Not funny, Sister Brendan. I found this in your storage "duka." Not only that but did you know that you have a rather good sized storage area under the building?"

"That's news to me. I've often wondered why they built such a solid storage shed when they rebuilt the mission after the war. I wished that they had spent more time and money on the surgery and the nurses' living quarters, but that was long before my time.

"Anyway, Brother Sebastian has always maintained our supplies. He inventories and stores everything except medicine that comes in. We keep the medical supplies in the dispensary. When we want something from storage we ask him. He gets it. He gets irritated if we get something ourselves. He says it messes up his system and records."

"Well, the storage area is deep enough for a six foot tall man to stand up in and has electricity. I dropped down in and there are a number of footlocker sized black containers. This package was lying on top of one of them."

"What were you doing there in the first place?"

"Sebastian's in Marsabit getting supplies. I was replacing the tools we borrowed. I went to put a fallen box on the shelf and noticed a trap door. Curiosity took over."

"Matt, this is serious. We're here at the sufferance of the Kenyan government. If the commissioner finds that we have weapons, we will be thrown out on our rosaries. This isn't the loveliest spot in the world but we're helping the people. They need us."

"Let's get Sebastian in here when he comes back and find out what he has to say. In the meantime, let me find out what is in the containers. Then we can have our talk with Sebastian. For the time being, we should keep this to ourselves."

"That shouldn't be too hard. There's only Sister Columba, Moses, and your driver around besides the Kenyans."

"When's Sebastian due back?"

"This evening."

"Good. That gives me time to find out what's down there. I'll take a look in his living quarters, too."

"No, I'd prefer you didn't. Sebastian's been here in the desert for over forty years. He hardly seems a conspirator. Let's hear what he has to say. I'm certain he has an explanation, but what it may be is beyond me for sure."

"How the hell can he have a reasonable explanation for this armory in the middle of the desert?" Matt muttered to himself. "I'll get some tools from the Rover and go down again when you reopen the clinic for the late afternoon session and everyone is busy. Don't send anyone to the storage shed while I'm there."

"I won't. Come here at six for tea and tell me what else we're storing. There's another complication."

"What?"

"The Vatican representative is coming for his semi-annual visit tomorrow. I got a radio message from Kamala."

"Didn't you know he was coming?"

"He's a month early."

"What's this all about?"

"Bureaucracy. Rome supports us financially and they send somebody out to inspect us twice a year."

"I thought your order in Ireland ran the mission."

"No. We just furnish the nuns."

"What's this guy do?"

"Not much, he usually stays a couple of days, chats with us and Brother Sebastian. He looks at our books and inventory records. He and Brother Sebastian walk around and inspect the buildings. He makes a list of anything special we need and leaves. He's not very personable."

"I'll get my snooping done before he gets here."

When the clinic reopened at three, Matt let himself into the shed, a substantial building approximately thirty by thirty square. The first floor was ten feet high with storage shelves along all of the walls and in the middle of the room. Matt thought it looked like an unusually well stocked Home Depot. Matt moved a large box to block the outside door in case someone came by. The trap door in the floor opened on well-oiled hinges. Obviously someone cared for it on a regular basis.

Dropping to the concrete floor, he turned on the light and moved over to the three black containers. They were about three feet by two feet. On the outside in Italian, English, French and German a label stated it was the property of the Vatican Diplomatic Corps. To Matt the other languages seemed to say the same as the English. They were addressed to His Excellency Bishop Sergio Pannatta, Nairobi Kenya.

The first one, unlocked and empty, had a padded interior divided into compartments. Trying to move the second one he discovered it was beyond his strength. The third moved more easily and Matt started to work on the Grubber lock with the tools he brought from the Rover. The lock did not respond to his hammer and screwdriver. However, the passage of time had taken its toll on the hinges and Matt, removing them easily, opened the locker.

It was half full of spools of what appeared to be insulated electrical wiring. The markings said the wire was a product of the SPAM Electrical Company, Milano, Italy and held 75 meters of wire. Curious about why seemingly ordinary electrical wiring would receive this special packing, Matt unrolled a couple of feet and sliced it with his knife. It cut more easily than he expected.

"Why do they need so much?" he wondered. He

noticed similarly marked spools of wire on the shelves on the first floor. He cut two more lengths of wire.

Matt replaced things as he had found them and returned to his quarters. He stripped off the orange insulation. It came off easily leaving Matt holding a yellow length of pliable metal that looked like gold.

"Gold?" His mind spun.

First guns and then gold hidden in a Catholic mission in the middle of a desert in Africa. This was more than he had bargained for. Was this what his friend Jay was talking about? His six o'clock tea with Sister Brendan would be very interesting.

Back in his room, Matt tried to read or sleep but his whirring mind kept him awake. He puzzled over the date of the Italian rebuilding, 1946, and the gold recalled the news reports of the gold stolen by the Nazi's and sent to Switzerland at the end of World War II. But there were no Germans around here. Even if there were, why was the gold in the middle of the desert and not in some bank in Europe? Was there a connection between this mission and Switzerland? Any connection seemed unlikely to him but then so was his discovery. He finally drifted off to a restless sleep.

He awoke in time to freshen up and arrive for tea promptly at six. Sister Brendan was already there. She poured the omnipresent tea and he helped himself to a biscuit.

"Well, Sister, did you know that you are probably the richest mission in West Africa?"

"Cut the nonsense, Matt. What did you find? What are you talking about?"

Matt handed over two pieces of the wire. Sister Brendan examined them with a quizzical look on her face. "If I didn't know better I'd say that this is gold. Is this what you found in the storage shed?"

"You bet and there's a lot more. There was probably much, much more once upon a time. What's this all about?"

Sister Brendan began pacing back and forth, sloshing her tea. Finally she stopped and shook her head. "I have no idea Matt. Do you have a guess?"

Matt leaned back in the sofa. "I don't know. But the weapons and the fact the shed was built just after the end of World War II makes me think it could be Nazi gold."

Sister Brenda took a seat opposite Matt and gave a look of disbelief. "Nazi gold? St. Patrick between us and all harm. The war ended over fifty years ago. There have been no Germans here at any time to my knowledge."

"A German was killed just last week in the district. Kamala said he was shot repeatedly with some type of automatic weapon like those in the package."

"Let's not get ahead of ourselves," Sister Brendan said. "Sebastian can give us some answers. We'll ask him when he gets back. We don't have any other choice."

"Yes we do. Turn everything over the commissioner. Let him handle it," Matt said leaning forward for emphasis.

"No," she said emphatically. "Not until we talk to Sebastian."

"Okay," Matt said rising from his seat. "But I want to look in his room to see if he has any more weapons. Our safety may be at stake."

"I don't believe that. Sebastian's a gentle person. But I have to admit that what you found makes me change my mind about a search. Go ahead."

Brother Sebastian's small room, attached to the warehouse, measured no more than fifteen by twenty feet, and looked like what Matt pictured as a monk's cell, maybe bigger, but just as sparse. Against the wall to his left, sat a narrow bed. Facing him was a desk with writing materials on its surface. In addition, he saw a comfortable looking old chair, a reading light, a footstool and a chest of drawers. The rest of the furnishings consisted of a small table and bookcases along the walls.

Narrow windows graced each of the three walls not attached to the warehouse. One overhead light and a lamp on the desk broke the dimness in the little room, and a sink in one corner dripped intermittently. Matt supposed that Sebastian used the toilet and shower in the clinic.

On the walls were a picture of the Pope, a crucifix and a picture of the Blessed Virgin. The bookcase contained the Bible and what appeared to be other religious books in Italian, German and English. Matt's quick look didn't reveal any secular books, nor were there any pictures of family.

A dedicated man, thought Matt, but with a question mark after it. Matt went through the drawers in the dresser and found nothing unusual. The drawers in the desk were also mostly empty. However, in the lower left hand drawer, not hidden, were four packets of letters.

Matt estimated about fifty or sixty of them. The first letter was dated in June 1946, and the last letter, December 1975. They bore no postage, so were apparently delivered by hand. They were addressed to a Bruno Facetta. Since they were hand-written in German, Matt had no way of knowing what they said. The salutation was to Lieben sohn, and signed, Mit liebe, Mutter. Above the date was written Klagenfurt. Matt put the last three in his pocket. He made sure everything was as it had been when he entered the room and left to look for Sister Brendan. He found her in the clinic and they went to the sitting room.

"As the walrus said 'It gets curiouser and curiouser.' I think it was the walrus. But this is very serious. Remember my reference to Nazi gold? Now we have a German connection. I thought you said that Sebastian was Italian?"

"He is, at least that's what he holds himself out to be. I have only heard him speak English and some of the local languages he has picked up. He speaks Italian with Father LoBretti when he comes to say Mass every ten days or two weeks. Sebastian's accent, when he speaks English, is like the Italian-English accent I heard from Italians when I visited Italy, but that was a long time ago," she sighed. "It looks like we have a lot to talk to Sebastian about."

"You bet."

"Let's have some tea while we wait," she said.

"What would you do without tea?"

"I don't know. It seems to be the universal lubricant of the Irish and English world."

Just after sundown an African came in and told them that Brother Sebastian had returned.

"Ask him to come in here please," Sister Brendan

looked as though she dreaded the task at hand. Matt could not blame her.

"I'll get the collection," Matt said.

Chapter 13

Sebastian's Story

Dressed in well-worn, many times washed khaki pants and shirt, Sebastian entered the room where Sister Brendan and Matt waited. His limp, more pronounced, betrayed his fatigue. That and exposure to the sun made his face look even older than his seventy-six years. But his active life, primarily vegetarian diet and abstinence from alcohol or tobacco left his body trim and wiry, far different from the usual image of the corpulent monks of the Middle Ages.

"Why did you want me?" he asked. "Is there a problem?"

"I'm afraid so, Sebastian," Sister Brendan said. "Matt has discovered something disturbing. I hope you can help us."

"I'll try."

Matt pulled a canvas bag from behind his chair. He slowly unwrapped the weapons and put them on the coffee table between them. Sebastian's face tightened.

"Wait," Matt said. He placed a length of wire with the gold partially exposed next to the weapons. Sebastian looked from Matt to Sister and back. Finally Matt laid down the letters he had taken from Sebastian's room. Sebastian put his head in his hands. His body rocked back and forth and a soft moan came from behind the hands.

Matt and Sister Brendan waited.

Sebastian composed himself, straightened and spoke to Sister Brendan. "What do you want of me? I'll be gone tomorrow if you want."

"It's not that simple," Matt snapped. "This is serious stuff. We need to contact the commissioner."

"Matt, relax," Sister Brendan said. "Brother Sebastian has been here for years. He's always been kind and gentle. Let him tell us what he knows. Then we can decide what we have to do."

"All right, but let's see if he has a weapon on him."

"I don't," Sebastian said in an almost inaudible voice.

"That's enough, Matt. What can you tell us, Sebastian? Where did these things come from? Why are they here?"

Sebastian began talking in a subdued voice. "First, I never did anything that would harm the mission or anyone here. What I did, I did to protect what was left of my family in Europe and later on to protect myself. I'd hoped to die before any of this matter became known. It's a long story."

"Let's hear it," Matt said belligerently.

"We have all night," Sister Brendan said sympathetically to her coreligious. "I've my own ghosts. Most stories are not as unpleasant as the tellers think."

Sister Brendan's tone relaxed Sebastian. He sat back in his chair and began. "First, I didn't get my limp in the war as people assume. I never corrected that assumption. I was born with it. It plays a part in my life and how I came to be here." He paused and sighed. "I'm not sure how to begin."

"Take your time, it'll come," Brendan said.

"Yes, go ahead," Matt urged in a softer voice.

"The letters from Klagenfurt are from my mother. She's been dead for sometime now. She was Austrian, my father Italian. We lived in the town of Talmezzo, not far from Cortina, close to both Austria and Yugoslavia. In the north of Italy and southern Austria the people move back and forth freely. Both my parents were avid skiers. They met before the war at one of the skiing areas, fell in love and married. Because they were such athletes, my being born a cripple affected their view of me. They weren't directly harsh or mean, but I wasn't held in the same affection as my brother and sister."

"What happened to your father?" Matt asked.

"He was a reserve officer with the Alpine troops. He was called up and in 1942 he was sent with the Italian 8th Army to the Russian front. We never heard from him again."

"I'm sorry," Matt said. "What happened to you?"

"In 1943, when the Axis started to lose the war, I'd been in the Army about two years. . ."

"How'd you get into the army with your limp?" Matt interrupted.

"Italy called up everyone. We had been fighting since the late thirties, in Africa, Greece and eventually Russia. By 1941 we were desperate for soldiers."

The questioning brought back things that Sebastian

hadn't thought about for years.

"What happened to the rest of your family?" Matt asked.

"They got overwhelmed by events. In January 1944 the Allies invaded. In July Mussolini was kicked out of office and killed. Italy surrendered and declared war on Germany. Then the Germans sent six more divisions into northern Italy. It was a mess. Mother had been a vocal backer of Hitler and, after the surrender, the villagers in Talmezzo harassed her and my brother and sister. For the family's safety she moved backed to Klagenfurt with my sister and brother. She wasn't bothered there, but living conditions were difficult."

"Where are your brother and sister?"

"My brother enrolled in one of the Werewolf groups the Nazis formed at the end of the war and he was killed fighting around Berlin. My sister married an Austrian and lives somewhere in Austria now. She thinks I'm dead."

"Okay, but what did you do in the Army?" Matt shifted impatiently in his chair.

"I was assigned to a military police unit. We guarded supply dumps and airports and directed traffic. It was easy and safe but that changed toward the end of the war.

"How?" Sister Brendan asked.

"In 1944, almost all German and Croatian troops in Croatia were sent to the Russian front. My unit was transferred to Croatia to replace them. My company was assigned to guard the Jasenovac Concentration camp set up by the fascist Ustashi Government of Croatia." Brother Sebastian, talking faster, was wringing his hands and breathing heavily.

"Slow down, relax, Sister Brendan said. "Would you like some water or something else?"

"Water would be fine, Sister."

She poured the water and handed it to him. During his recital he had moved up in the chair until he was sitting on the front edge leaning forward, poised as if ready to spring. As he sipped the water he relaxed back into the chair.

"Sorry for the rush of words. This memory is very disturbing. It's been eating at my soul for over fifty years. I couldn't even go to Confession."

"So far I haven't heard anything that you did that was so bad. Seems they were just moving you around." Matt said. "Anything else happen?"

"The camp. I couldn't stand what I saw every day. Six thousand prisoners, always the worst conditions. Only a few lived very long after they arrived. If they didn't die of starvation or disease they were hung, shot, or worse."

"I know about the camps in Germany and Poland. Who was in your camp?"

"Jews. Serbs. Gypsies. Anyone the Croatian Fascist government didn't like. I was going crazy watching them die."

"Did you have direct contact with them?"

"No. All I had to do was walk the fence to see that no one escaped, as if any were strong enough. But I felt I was killing them. We didn't have a chaplain so I went to talk to my Captain, Beppe Orsini. He had been a friend of my father. After he was wounded in Africa he was made the commander of the guard unit near our town while he recovered."

"What'd you expect him to do?" Sister Brendan asked.

Sebastian felt his gut tighten as he remembered his visit with the captain. Staring at the ceiling, he was back in Croatia fifty years ago.

ↄ৪   ↄ৪   ↄ৪

"Captain, I can't stand this. I can't sleep. Let's turn our guns on the Croatians, set the prisoners free and go home."

"I share your feelings. Others have come to me with the same fears. But, as commander of the unit, it's my job to get as many of you home safely as I can. Attacking the Croatians is the last thing we should do. Even if we free the prisoners they're too weak to go far. They'll be hunted down or starve. They're better off where they are. Besides, we're over 100 kilometers from Trieste. We'd be killed before we got out of Croatia. We'd never get home and we wouldn't be helping the prisoners."

"Can't we do something?"

"The war's almost over. The Russians are in Hungary, the Allies in Venice and Rome. Let's stay together as a unit, gather supplies, protect our trucks and, at the first sign the guards are nervous show the commandant our orders to return to Italy and we'll take off."

"Do you have orders?"

"No, Bruno, but I'll have them as soon as our company clerk finishes forging them," Orsini said with a slight smile. "Be careful, be silent and be ready. We could move at anytime. We don't want to be caught here by the Allies."

One evening, a couple of weeks later, the platoon sergeant came into the barracks. "Facetta, Barbieri, the Captain wants you, in uniform, in his office in twenty minutes," he barked. The men looked up from their reading. In response to puzzled looks the sergeant added, "I don't know why but we've got visitors."

"I hope it has something to do with going home before the Americans occupy all Italy," Barbieri said.

The men reported and the Captain's aide motioned them into the briefing room. Captain Orsini stood at the front of the room. Seated at the table were a German Colonel, a Croatian Captain, and a man dressed as a priest. Six other solders from the unit were there standing at attention.

"At ease. Seats," Orsini ordered.

"This is bad," Sebastian thought. The presence of the German officer was ominous. As if the thought had cued him the German stood and spoke. "Italy has surrendered. The German army has been ordered to disarm and send to Germany for imprisonment all members of the Italian Army. You're our prisoners. My men have secured your weapons in the storehouse."

The Italians looked at each other and murmured.

"Quiet," the Colonel and Captain Orsini said as one.

Bruno looked at his Captain. "Is this true?"

"Unfortunately, yes."

The soldiers looked around and saw two German soldiers armed with Schmeisser assault rifles in the back of the room.

"However, all may not be lost for you. You've been called here because your Captain tells me that you all speak fluent German. Ja? Nien?"

"Ja, Herr Oberst," the men replied.

"Good. We have a proposal for you."

The Croatian officer stood. "There are those among us Croatians a group known as Krizaris, Crusaders, who intend to continue this war against godless communism. The Russians are in Budapest raping and pillaging. We're taking the treasures of the Croatian Church out of their way and out of the grasp of their henchman, Tito. Icons, chalices, vestments and other Church treasures are to be taken to Rome for safe-keeping and to finance our resistance. As we speak, those items are being assembled in Ljubljana and other cities. As good Catholics you should be happy to help us."

"Why should we? We're prisoners," Barbieri said.

"Not if you do as you're told."

"What?"

"The German Army can't spare men to move the goods and Croatians driving across Italy is not a good idea. You men speak German. You'll act as German guards and help us get to Rome."

"Our incentive?" someone asked.

"When you finish you can go home and not spend the rest of the war in a prison camp in Germany."

"Why can't we go as Italian soldiers?"

"First, you could be captured by other German units, and our orders, as high as they are, probably can't protect you. Secondly, the partisans, mostly communists, are growing bolder in the north and they're more likely to attack an Italian unit than a German one."

"If we refuse?"

"Prison, execution, who knows?"

"We need to talk to our Captain," Barbieri said.

The German and the Croat looked at each other. The German nodded. "Ten minutes." They left the room.

When the door closed the men all spoke at once.

"Quiet," Captain Orsini commanded. "This is still a military unit." He pointed to another soldier. "You first."

"What can we do?"

"Not much. The Germans who moved in today are heavily armed. They've got our weapons. We can accept their offer or be shot or, at best, go to prison camp. I think we should accept the offer or I wouldn't have brought you here. They apparently have the authority to get us to Rome."

"What about the church things they're taking?"

"The Croat has a good story but my impression is that this is a deal between the Nazis and the Croat fascists, the Ustashi. From what they let slip there may also be gold from the Central Bank that they are going to 'protect' from the Communists. My view is that if this were one hundred percent legitimate they'd use German troops. Any more questions?"

"I don't think we have a choice. I think they'll kill us if we refuse," Bruno said.

"I agree," Captain Orsini replied. The other men nodded.

Orsini invited the others back into the room. "We agree."

"Wise decision," the German said. "Get your personal gear and report to the motor pool in thirty minutes. Say nothing to anyone."

The priest, who had been silent until now, rose and spoke. "Pardon my Italian. It's been many years since I studied in Rome. You should be happy that you're doing God's work. A special relationship, going back seven hundred years, exists between the Vatican and Croatia. Croatia is the frontier of Christianity against the godless hordes from the east. When you complete this mission you will be rewarded both in Heaven and on earth. Kneel."

Bemused, the soldiers knelt. The priest prayed in Latin and made the Sign of the Cross over them.

"Dominus vobiscum," he concluded. The Italians blessed themselves in response."

"Go," Orsini ordered.

The men gathered their personal gear and assembled at the motor pool. They climbed into a waiting Opel "Blitz" truck and, following a VW Kubelwagen carrying the Colonel, the Captain and the Croatian, set out on the first lap of the journey.

As the two-vehicle convoy approached the southern outskirts of Ljubljana, it turned off on a side road and in two kilometers entered a German military compound. Waived through the gate, the truck stopped in front of a gray, low slung barracks.

Captain Orsini arrived at the back of the truck. "Inside quickly," he ordered. Waiting inside was a six-foot-four, blond German Sergeant.

"Form a rank," he ordered. "I'm Feldwebel Wagner.

I'm in charge of this operation. I didn't request this assignment and I don't like it. Try to act like soldiers. It'll be easier for all of us. Line up."

The soldiers formed up. "Take off everything including watches and chains. Fold your clothes in front of you. Put all other personal belongings in a pile in front of your clothes."

The soldiers who remembered similar procedures at the prison camp, froze.

"Don't make this difficult." Wagner rested his right hand on the Mauser pistol strapped to his side. The Italians complied. "Pick up your new uniforms, underwear, socks and boots from the piles at the end of the room."

The men relaxed a little.

"Your personal items will be given to your Captain and returned when the mission is over. Make sure the uniforms fit. You're supposed to be German soldiers, not some Italian rabble."

With much trying on and exchange of clothes, the Italians finally were fitted out in dark green field blouses with the white service color of the German infantry, and matching trousers. Wagner inspected each man in his new uniform and declared them passable. Just as they were finishing, Orsini appeared in a German officer's uniform.

"Bruno, your German is the least accented. You're in charge. Speak only German. Stay here. Food's coming."

A few hours later Wagner reappeared. He took the Italians to a firing range and gave them brief instructions in the use of old bolt action Mauser rifles. Each fired five rounds. The results were not impressive.

After dark, Bruno and his companions were back in their truck. A short ride further into the woods brought them to a open area where four Mercedes Benz trucks with German markings and drivers waited.

"There are rifles in the first truck. Each take one," Orsini ordered. "I want one man in front with the driver and one man in the back with the cargo. Move."

The men in the back of the trucks saw tarpaulins. The curious who looked under the coverings saw wooden crates with no markings.

Orsini got into the Kubelwagen with the driver, the German Colonel and Croatian officer. The convoy moved west along the main road to Trieste. Thirty kilometers later they turned onto a smaller road meandering northwest and eventually arrived in the town of Koabrid. After a rest stop they took an even less traveled road southwest toward Udine, Italy. The convoy covered five more kilometers before halting at a border crossing manned by an officer and two guards. Instead of waiting, the Colonel jumped down and went inside the guard shack. Orsini saw him showing papers to the guards. He returned immediately and the trucks proceeded with no inspection.

"The guards said that the main roads should be secure, but that there has been increased partisan activity. Italian deserters have joined the partisans in the mountains further west and they have gotten bolder. Be alert."

"Yes, Sir," the driver said.

The vehicles moved slowly without incident to Udine where they picked up the major highway toward Venice.

The traffic, almost exclusively military, was light. Using nightlights and maintaining the proper spacing and moderate speed, they proceeded through the night.

"Before we get to Venice we'll turn on the road marked by signs to Padua and Verona. We'll bypass Verona on the south," the colonel directed the driver.

"Yes, Sir."

About two in the morning as the convoy approached the bridge over the Adige River they saw dim lights ahead.

"Stop." The Colonel looked at the activity through his night glasses.

"German soldiers manning a road block. Shouldn't be a problem but let's be cautious. Drive to a hundred meters from the barricade then stop on the side of the road."

When they stopped, the colonel again surveyed the roadblock through his glasses. "There's something strange. They're blocking the road with only a staff car and a truck. Wagner, come with me. Let's see what's going on."

The Kubelwagen moved slowly toward the roadblock. They saw no other traffic. The driver pulled up ten meters from the barricade. When the Colonel and the Sergeant dismounted they could see two trucks blocking the traffic from the opposite direction but with only two soldiers in view. The placement of the trucks required traffic to slow and make an S curve to proceed.

As the Germans approached the blockade, a lieutenant and two enlisted men armed with rifles stepped forward to meet them. The Germans could now see other armed soldiers behind the vehicles.

The lieutenant saluted. "Sorry to delay you, Sir. We're looking for Italian deserters and weapons that may be going to the partisans."

"Admirable, Lieutenant. I assure you that we have neither of those in our trucks so there is no need to delay us."

"Yes, Sir, but I have strict orders to search all vehicles."

"Certainly not vehicles of the Wehrmacht on an official mission."

"My orders say all vehicles, Sir."

"Let me talk to your commanding officer."

"He was called back to camp. I'm in charge."

"Here are my orders signed by General Wolffe's Chief of Staff. I suggest that you let us pass. In fact, I order you to let us pass."

"After we search the trucks, Sir. If you'll have them move up one at a time it should only take a few minutes."

The two officers stared into each other's eyes. The soldiers behind the lieutenant fingered their rifles. Sergeant Wagner kept his hands at his side but his eyes scrutinized the soldiers and the vehicles.

Finally, the colonel spoke. "I admire your obedience to orders. You'll go far--unless my report on your insubordination in the face of a direct order gets you court-martialed."

"Yes, Sir. Please move your trucks slowly forward to the barricade. After we search one it can go through and we'll check the others."

"I'll order my men," the Colonel said.

The lieutenant saluted. The Colonel returned it and walked back toward the Volkswagen.

"What did you notice, Sergeant?" The Colonel asked.

"That's not a German army unit. They have the wrong vehicles for a blockade. The officer is not of sufficient rank, and I didn't see any automatic weapons, only rifles."

"We should be happy for that."

"One of the riflemen had a supply corps insignia on his right sleeve. Guess they forgot to take it off."

"Assemble the drivers at the end of the convoy. Tell the Italians to get in the back of the trucks and keep out of sight. I am sure they don't want to be found in German uniforms by their fellow Italians."

When the German drivers had assembled, the colonel said, "There's a lightly armed unit blocking the road. I'm convinced they're partisans. They apparently have only rifles but I don't want to try shooting our way through. We'll run their blockade. Sergeant, drive the first truck. We'll have a soldier with an automatic weapon with you. Drive up slowly and when you get within twenty meters accelerate. Don't accelerate very quickly, but your guard will start firing at the same time you speed up and the surprise should get you through. Then I want you to try to sideswipe the end vehicle of the second barricade. It should create enough confusion to get us through."

He turned to the other drivers. "You, accelerate as the first truck approaches the barricade. Move as fast as you can through the curve. Captain Orsini and I will be in the third and fourth trucks. The Kubelwagen stays right behind the third truck, it should give it some protection.

When you get through, go twenty kilometers down the road and stop. Get ready to fire on pursuers but I don't think there'll be any." The drivers saluted and manned their trucks.

The Sergeant eased the big Mercedes truck toward the opening on the left side of the road. Three men in German uniforms blocked the way and signaled where the truck should stop. When the sergeant was about fifteen meters from the men he shifted gears and accelerated. The soldier in the passenger seat aimed his weapon down the line formed by the two blockading vehicles and sprayed it with bursts of automatic fire.

The partisans in front of the oncoming truck dove for safety. Others got off a few wild shots while ducking for cover. The spray of fire from the truck kept them from aiming. The German truck, hit by a few bullets in the side and back sustained little damage. The heavy truck picked up enough speed so that when it clipped the end of the lighter truck blocking the road ahead, the lighter truck slid sideways and scattered the men around it. The big Mercedes continued on its way.

The second truck was not as lucky. A few of the partisans in the second rank, whether by luck or skill, hit its front left tire with their fire. When the driver tried to turn the vehicle left through the curve, it skidded into the blockading vehicles in the second line and turned on it side. As the passengers, including the Croatian Captain, jumped out of the back, they were shot down as they tried to surrender.

With attention focused on the disabled vehicle, the other two trucks and the Kubelwagen were able to dash through the blockade without taking any serious damage. The vehicles rendezvoused as planned.

"Good work, Sergeant. Take a damage survey."

A few minutes later Wagner reported. "We lost the driver, two Italians and the Croatian with the second truck. No injuries to the other men, Sir. We've taken a few bullet holes and some damaged windshields. The Kubelwagen was protected behind the truck and it came through in good shape."

"Nothing we can do about the lost truck. Let's move out. They'll be busy trying to loot it and figure out how they're going to get into the mountains before someone else arrives."

"If I had five men I could go back and finish them off."

"I'm sure you could, Sergeant, but we don't have time to spare from our mission. Let's get to Milan."

In the early dawn, no one paid attention to the battle-scarred convoy as it moved slowly through the streets of the industrial area of north Milan. One of the Italian soldiers was familiar with Milan and, with the aid of a map, guided the vehicles to their destination, a large commercial warehouse.

"Tap your horn three times," the Colonel directed. In response, a workman looked from inside the warehouse. The huge industrial doors opened and the trucks were directed to a loading dock at the back of the warehouse.

"We're staying here tonight and then we'll return to Trieste and take most of the Italians with us," the Colonel told Wagner. "Follow the workman and get the men settled."

Wagner and the soldiers followed to a loft room with pallets on the floor. "Make yourselves comfortable. We'll be here for twenty-four hours."

The Germans gathered at one end of the room, the Italians at the other. Food, magazines, blankets and smoking materials were brought but the soldiers spent most of their time sleeping or talking quietly among themselves.

During the day, the cargo from the three remaining trucks was loaded into one large trailer truck with the markings of an Italian commercial trucking company on its side.

Early the next morning, Wagner reappeared in the loft with two men carrying civilian clothing similar to the clothes worn by the workers in the warehouse. They dumped them in the middle of the floor.

"Get dressed in these," Wagner ordered the Italians. He dropped a cloth sack. "Here are your valuables. When you're dressed, go down stairs. Take your uniforms with you and put them in the first truck."

Wagner told the German drivers to man their vehicles.

When the Italians came down, they saw Captain Orsini dressed in civilian clothes and moved to him.

"Men, your part of the mission is over. Facetta and I will accompany the shipment to Rome. The Germans are returning to their unit near Trieste. They'll take you there and give you passes to get to your homes. Good luck." They exchanged salutes. He turned and walked with Facetta to the large transport.

"Pick up water and rations from the table behind you

and get in the second truck," Wagner ordered the five Italians.

A half hour later, the commercial vehicle wended its way westward through the streets of Milan, toward the highway to Genoa. At the same time, heading east, the German vehicles were entering the main highway to Trieste.

Two hours outside of Milan, the colonel ordered the driver to pull over next to a lay-by.

"Sergeant, tell the men we'll take a fifteen minute break. If they have to relieve themselves or want a smoke go back in the trees out of the sight of the road. I don't want anyone worrying about what civilians are doing in Army trucks. Then come back."

"Yes, Sir."

The sergeant relayed the orders. The men drifted off into the woods, the Germans in one group and the Italians in another.

Wagner returned. "Sergeant, get your men and cleanse the area then we can go on. I'm going down the road and have a cigarette." He turned and strolled off.

Five minutes later the Colonel heard the sounds of weapons fire. First a fusillade, then five isolated shots. He finished his cigarette and walked slowly back to his truck. The sergeant stood by the first truck. He saluted. "Sir, the area is clean and secure. Our men are back in their truck."

"Good, let's go." The trucks pulled back onto the road and continued towards Trieste.

ଓଃ   ଓଃ   ଓଃ

"Brother, let's take a break. Does anybody want anything?" Matt asked.

Sister and Sebastian said they'd like fresh tea. While Matt was warming the pot and heating the water Brendan and Sebastian excused themselves to use the bathrooms.

Matt wondered: Where is this story going? What the hell are we in the middle of?

Sebastian rubbed cold water over his face and the inside of his wrists to cool himself. When he returned to the sitting room, the cups had been refreshed. Matt and Sister Brendan had returned to their chairs. Sebastian took his cup, sipped his tea, added some lemon, and continued.

"In Milan, the Captain and I changed into clerical outfits supplied by the priest. That was where I first became a Brother," Sebastian said ironically. "We were given papers identifying us as officials of the Vatican Diplomatic Corps bringing food supplies to the Holy City. When we got to Genoa we drove into a large warehouse in the port area. The truck was stored under armed guard.

"We went to a nearby church where we stayed in the priest's residence until the city was under allied control and some type of order prevailed. Eventually our cargo was loaded onto a ship bound for Rome. By this time, the Captain and the priest had convinced me that I should stay with them because if we were captured by the Allies, the captain and I would be arrested. Besides we were now doing the Lord's work, the priest insisted, and I believed him, probably because I had no other choice. We arrived in the port near Rome and passed through security with no problem.

"We, and the boxes, were taken to the Pontifico Santa Maria dell'Anima, one of the three seminaries for German priests in Rome. I never saw the boxes or the priest who accompanied us again."

"What happened to you?"

"Captain Orsini and I were taken to an office and interviewed by a man dressed like a priest."

"Did you have any reason to think he wasn't?" Matt asked.

"No. He said he was Father Peter and that we were to make ourselves at home until arrangements could be made for us to go to another country. Captain Orsini thanked the priest but said he'd like to go back to his family when it was safe. Father Peter said that the Captain would be given documents that would get him get back to his town but he had to swear on the bones of Saint Francis that he'd never reveal any details of the trip. They didn't want the Communists to learn about the art treasures, chalices, and the like that we had brought from Croatia. That was the first I knew of what we brought. Captain Orsini said he would tell no one."

"What about you?" Sister Brendan asked.

"I told the priest my father was dead and my mother, brother and sister were in Austria. I had no desire to go to Austria and live under the British occupation authorities who could know of my connection with Jasenovac. The priest suggested I stay in Rome for the time being. I could work with the Brothers in the seminary and brush up on my English that I had studied in school. I could also start studying Spanish in case I went to South America someday. This was a new thought to me, but I agreed."

"What'd you do in Rome?"

"Worked as a waiter, busboy and general cleaner in the guest house."

"Who were the guests?"

"Mostly German with some Austrians, Polish and Croatians. Usually there were thirty to forty men."

"War criminals?"

"Maybe."

"Did you do anything besides work?"

"Studied and participated in the religious exercises with the other Brothers, both German and Italian."

"Didn't you go out?" Matt asked.

"I walked around Rome on my day off with some of the Brothers. I loved going to the Vatican and the Sistine Chapel. Rome is beautiful. Sometimes I'd sit at a cafe, look at the young people and think I was one of them. I'd think of my brother and sister and what our life would have been like without the war."

"How did you end up here?" Sister Brendan asked.

"God's will. There was an elderly Italian priest, the spiritual director of the Brothers. One day I went to him and told him my story, my horror at what I had seen and my fear of being arrested. He was a great comfort. He said that he had lived during two great wars, the civil war in Spain, and the Russian revolution. He still couldn't understand the inhumanity of man to man, but believed that God's love would not be denied. We should keep trying to be good despite what was going on around us. He assured me there was no fault on my part. He told me to keep my faith in God and peace of mind and soul would come.

"Though I hadn't followed the formula of Confession, he gave me absolution. He recommended I continue following the Order's rules even though I was not a professed Brother. He said if I was given the chance to go to South America I should think hard before doing it because it would tie me forever with the fugitives."

Sister Brendan leaned forward. "Sebastian, that explains a lot but you still haven't told us about the gold or how you got here."

"It's late. I'm worn out by calling back all these bad memories. Can I rest and finish in the morning?"

"Normally I wouldn't have a problem with that but this is so serious I'd like to know it all I can before we go to sleep. After all, you may be gone in the morning," Matt said.

Sebastian's head pivoted toward Matt. Before he could speak Sister Brendan said, "I don't think that's a problem, Matt, I've known Sebastian for a long time. I'm sure he won't do anything to endanger or embarrass us. Besides there aren't a lot of places he can go."

"It's all right, Sister. If he wants to know I'll tell him. I'll try to make it short and if Matt has any questions he can ask me in the morning. I'll be here."

As mild as it was, Matt felt the rebuke.

Sebastian continued. "One day Padre Francis, the elderly priest, called me to his office. He said that the Congregation for the Propagation of the Faith was sending a team of craftsmen to work on the Vatican embassy in Nairobi and some churches in Kenya, including this one. They hadn't been able to get into Kenya since the beginning of World War II when the

English and Italians fought in Somalia. He pretty much ordered me to join the work group. He suggested I stay in Kenya to be out of Europe, South America or other places where the war criminals were hiding.

"The work team traveled with Vatican passports and had diplomatic immunity during the work. If I decided to stay there I could get a residence permit. Rome was also sending a full shipment of tools, building materials and equipment to rebuild and improve the embassy and churches. A survey team had already compiled a list of things we were to bring along. After some prayer and reflection I decided to go."

"Were you ever professed as a Brother?" Sister Brendan asked.

"Not formally. The Padre and I discussed it in case I wanted to stay and work as a Brother. He said don't worry about the formality of it. I had been living the life of a Brother for some time. He said if it meant anything to me, he thought I was a Brother by desire, just like baptism of desire. To qualm my conscience he went through the profession and vows with me. Then just to keep things straight, he said that he would see if some of his friends who were making documents for the Nazi's could slip a notation of my profession in the Order's official records. He thought it would be a good joke."

"Maybe not good but certainly poetic," Matt said.

"So I came to Africa with the work team. First we repaired the embassy in Nairobi. Then came up here. We rebuilt the church, expanded the clinic and put in the storage shed to hold supplies, but I didn't see any guns. Those came later with one of the Vatican visitors.

Anyway, I liked the manual labor and became friends with the nuns who were here then. They urged me to stay. I was still afraid of going home and really had nothing to go to, so I stayed."

"Didn't anyone back in Rome ever question your legitimacy?" Matt asked.

"Not that I knew about. If they did, Padre Francis handled it. After he died I was already integrated into the system."

"Matt," Sister Brendan said," that's enough for now. I'm exhausted and I need to digest what I've been told. Sebastian's not going anywhere. Let's talk about this tomorrow after the first clinic. Say some prayers for guidance, both of you."

Matt saw that Sister Brendan was firm about ending. "Okay, Sister. This is a pretty amazing story. I'm not sure what its effect will be on all of us. It deserves thought for sure. I'm not certain that telling Kamala about this will help anything. See you in the morning. Good night Sebastian."

"Good night, Sister. "Good night, Matt." Sebastian said.

After Sebastian left, Matt got up and paced the floor. He turned abruptly to Sister Brendan. "He hasn't told us a damn thing about why the weapons and the gold are here. We're right in the middle of something dangerous and we don't know what it is."

"I know. I'm as concerned as you are. Besides our personal safety the mission could be in trouble. But we can't do anything else tonight. He was exhausted and I didn't want him to get defensive. We need to know everything so we can decide what to do."

"How does this Monsignor Juraj fit into this? He can't be good news. If he's one of the bad guys we need to protect ourselves."

"Hopefully, we'll find out everything in the morning."

On that wishful note they parted.

Chapter 14

Monsignor Juraj

Next morning, after the first clinic, Sister Brendan and the men gathered in the common room with their ever-present cups of tea and a large teapot on the table between them. Sebastian was calmer and he managed a smile for his two confidants.

After they had settled themselves, Matt said, "Sebastian, you tell an intriguing story but where'd the gold come from? And the guns?"

"I'll tell you what I know. When we came to Kenya after the war we had a lot more material than we needed. The people in charge explained it away by saying that there was a scarcity of building materials and supplies because of the war so we had to bring things for the future with us. Better too much than too little. We could always store or sell the surplus. That made sense. We did sell a lot of materials but we stored spools of wire up here. There were three large spools, four or five feet high when standing on their sides. There were three hundred of the twenty kilo spools like what you found in the storage shed."

"Did they say why there was so much wire?"

"The only reason I ever heard was that we might

need to lay wire out to the buildings for electrical service or something of the sort."

"How did you find out it was gold?"

"After I decided to stay here I went to Nairobi to get my residence permit. One day as I was having lunch at the sidewalk restaurant of the New Stanley Hotel, a stranger sat down at my table."

ᘓ   ᘓ   ᘓ

"Hello, Bruno Facetta," a man said in Italian as he slid into the chair opposite Sebastian.

"Do I know you?"

"Don't be concerned. I just want to tell you about your extra duties. I come from your friends in Rome."

"What friends?"

"The friends who helped you get out of Croatia and housed and fed you in Rome. The extra duty is simple and won't interfere with your other work."

"Is it religious?"

"Some might think so. Listen, certain of the spools of electrical wire in your storage area bear a distinctive marking. The wire on these spools is gold. You're to safeguard them."

Sebastian sat up straight. He resisted the impulse to leave. "What? That's incredible."

"Not really. Some of it is the gold you helped smuggle out of Croatia. We figure you'd want to continue your job of keeping it safe."

"Ridiculous. We brought out items owned by the Church. Icons. Vestments. To keep them out of the hands of the Communists."

"Well, some of it was, but some of it was gold from the Central Bank and some of it was given to us by the people before they went into the camps. Gold we need to finance our struggles after the war."

Sebastian shuddered as the vision of the wretched people in the camps came back to him along with the thought of how the gold might have been *given*.

The man continued. "We found out in Rome that our gold was to be used to smuggle Germans to South America and set them up in business. We didn't take it to help the Germans. We want it to help our own and to keep our ideals alive until the people in Europe embrace them again, and they will. So we decided to send as much as we could out of Europe for later use. This project was ideal."

"What do you want me to do?"

"Not much. Watch it and turn it over only to people who have the password that we give you. You won't have many visitors. The desert and your activities will be the best guards."

"If I refuse?"

"Then the British Authorities in Kenya will apprehend a notorious escaped Italian war criminal. Your mother and sister in Austria might have some visitors too."

"I won't fight to protect it."

"We didn't think you would but you're the best we can do. We can't put anyone else at the mission. Besides no one else would want to stay there. Once a year or so, someone will visit the mission from Rome. He or someone in his group will be our representative. When he gives you the password let him take as much of the gold wire as he wants. Do your duty, you're still a soldier. The first password is Christ and Croatia."

The man rose and walked down the crowded Nairobi street.

Sebastian ran the conversation back and forth in his mind. He rationalized that he wouldn't have to do anything that he wasn't going to do before except let someone take something he didn't want anything to do with anyway. So he kept quiet and came back to the mission.

ↂ   ↂ   ↂ

"Where did the guns come from?" Sister Brendan asked.

"They're new. A couple of years ago we had two Austrian visitors at the mission. They said they were anthropologists. We get a number of them studying the tribes. Most of our visitors only stay one night but they stayed a few days. One day I found them in the supply building but they didn't find the cellar. I told them to stay out."

"What happened then?"

"Nothing, but I told the next person who came to pick up the gold and he left these guns. That was four or five years ago and I've never unwrapped them."

"So how does Juraj fit into the picture?"

"He started coming here about five or six years ago. Before that it was different people every two or three

172

years. They didn't come every year. They had the password so I gave them access to the storage cellar. When they left there was always less wire."

"How much did they take?"

"I don't know. At first they cut lengths off the big spools. The wire was very thick, like cable. When the big cable was gone they started taking a few spools at a time."

"As I recall the spools are marked twenty kilos a piece, that's forty-four pounds."

"That's right."

Matt took a pencil out of his pocket and started scribbling on a piece of paper. "If the gold is eighty to ninety percent of that weight, each spool holds thirty-five pounds of gold. When I retired I played around with some gold stocks. I think gold was selling about $250 to $270 an ounce then. You'd have to convert to troy ounces but those spools could be worth $125,000 to $150,000 each. Ten of those a year is a nice income."

Sister Brendan interrupted. "That's all very interesting, but what are we going to do about Juraj? He's supposed to be here this afternoon."

"There's not a lot we can do," Matt said. "We sure as heck can't confront him. He's probably armed and none of us are experienced with weapons."

"Even if we were, what would we do with him and his driver if we captured them? I can't see driving to Marsabit and telling Kamala this story," Brendan said. "I suggest that we go through this visit as in the past. Let him take his gold. When he's gone we'll have time to decide what to do. If we tell Kamala, he can have Juraj picked up in Nairobi. It's the safest way for us."

Sebastian and Matt agreed.

"Fine," Brendan said. "Sebastian, make sure everything is back in place, including the guns. We'll open the clinic this afternoon as usual. Matt, you and Moses can take another scout around the area. Sebastian can go with you."

"Done," Matt said and Sebastian nodded agreement. The three separated.

Ↄ Ↄ Ↄ

Monsignor Juraj and his driver pulled up to the clinic doorway as Sister Brendan opened it for its afternoon session. She walked out to the vehicle. "Monsignor, welcome. Why don't you clean up and rest from your dusty ride? You know where the guest quarters are. We'll meet in the refectory at seven o'clock for dinner."

"Fine, I can read my breviary but I'd like to talk to Brother Sebastian."

"Sebastian is on a drive with the visiting American." Sister told Juraj about the visitors and their mission. "They'll join us for dinner."

"I look forward to meeting them. I need my driver to look for the cause of some strange sounds coming from our vehicle. We noticed them on the drive from Marsabit. Could I have a key to the storage shed in case we need some spare parts?"

Sister couldn't see how she could refuse. She complied but reminded him to have his man lock the door after each use.

Matt, Sebastian and Moses walked into the refectory at seven.

"Monsignor, this is Matt Stark and his associate Moses Mrabi. They're doing a survey of the area for their American company."

Matt looked over the cleric, a tall and slender man with black hair, a small beard and dark, piercing eyes. What was unusual was that he was dressed in a modified clerical garb of black pants and black tunic with a cross hanging from a silver chain around his neck. Black clothing or clerical clothing, even modified, was usually not seen outside Nairobi.

The Monsignor nodded curtly in Sebastian's direction and extended his hand to Matt. The handshake was perfunctory. He didn't acknowledge the Kenyan.

"Pleasure to meet you," Matt said.

"Thank you."

Matt thought the Monsignor looked familiar but he couldn't place him. Besides, he reminded himself again that lots of people were looking familiar as he moved further into his sixties.

"Commissioner Kamala tells me that you are looking for oil in the desert and that you have done so before," the Monsignor said.

Juraj's voice sounded vaguely familiar to Matt. "More or less, Monsignor. We looked for oil about five or six years ago. I'm back in Kenya to talk to the government for another group who wants to do some work up here. While I was here, my group asked me to look at the area and check old water well sites and the airstrip. We drove into the desert about twenty miles from here and poked around."

"Poking around a desert does not sound too exciting. Did you and Brother Sebastian find anything?"

"Nothing of interest. The landing strip, or what we think was the strip, has been covered and uncovered by nature a few hundred times and is just another piece of desert. We had hoped to find a few pieces of metal that could have been old water wellheads to help us position our water wells if we decide to drill in the same place. That's about all."

Sister Brendan gestured toward the table set with china for dinner. "Monsignor Juraj, will you sit down and say Grace?" Monsignor Juraj said the formal "Bless us, O Lord" grace known to all Catholic children, a blessedly short prayer. This brevity was one of the benefits of the pre Vatican II Church, thought Sister Brendan.

The meal, prepared by local cooks assisted by the nuns, was flavorful. They served some of the meat, vegetables and staples Monsignor Juraj had brought from Nairobi. Thanks to his supplies, this meal was a considerable improvement from their usual rice and greens supplemented by goat and camel meat.

The businesslike dinner conversation centered on the work of the mission and dispensary. Monsignor Juraj, as Inspector for the Congregation of the Propagation of the Faith in Rome, talked about his group. They supported missions such as this around the world, and received reports on the missions' activities.

Sister Columba then read off the statistics of all the people they had treated over the last year. Juraj showed visible irritation when she read out the number of converts in the last year, a total of three. All three of these were nomads who for one reason or another came to work in the mission.

"It sounds to me," Juraj said, "that these are what they used to call in the Chinese missions 'Rice Christians.' They only convert because they want to be fed and clothed."

Sister Brendan sighed. This issue came up every visit. Trying to hide her irritation she said, "That may be true Monsignor, but our soul-o-meter is broken. We can't tell why these people want to be baptized, so if they study the lessons and say the words we baptism them."

"That's enough, Sister," Juraj said angrily. "You've been told that if you can't make converts we can't keep the mission open. The business of the Church is to save souls, not give away medicine randomly. I don't know why we've kept the mission open as long as we have."

Yes, you do, you hypocrite, Brendan thought. Then she said out loud, "Sorry, Monsignor, I thought taking care of these people was performing the corporal works of mercy I had been taught all my life. It was something that Christ did when He was on earth."

The Monsignor rose abruptly. "Thank God for His meal," he said.

"I need to write up a report of today's findings," Moses said, excusing himself from the table and leaving the room.

The Monsignor said, "Sister, the conversation has been most enlightening. Now I must talk to Brother Sebastian. I have instructions for him from his superiors in Rome. Brother, let's go to your quarters."

"I don't think so, Monsignor," Sebastian said.

"You don't understand me, Brother. I have orders from Rome." Then he said in German, "Get to your room."

The sound of the German activated Matt's memory. Suddenly, in Matt's mind, Monsignor Juraj's beard disappeared. He recognized the piercing eyes. Juraj had been the man in Wolffe's office in Vienna. A shock went through his body.

"No," Sebastian said. "I've told Sister Brendan and Mr. Stark about my background. I've told them about the gold."

Matt and Sister Brendan's heads turned from side to side as they watched the tense faces of the two men. Sister Columba sat dumbfounded as the confrontation ignited.

"Brother, you talk too much."

"Why all the secrecy? I was told the gold was going to support Nazis who had stayed in San Gerolomo and moved overseas."

"Yes," Juraj snapped, "and it supports our cause in Germany and Austria, but that's none of their business."

"Your cause is dead and discredited," Matt said.

"You're out of touch. Read the election returns from Europe. Read about our fight to keep the undesirables out of Europe."

"You support those fascists and skin heads?" Matt said.

"They serve a purpose." Juraj's expression became dark. "I'm afraid Brother that you have put your friends in an awkward position."

Monsignor Juraj slipped a Walther PP pistol from inside his loose tunic. "By now my driver should have loaded most of the remaining gold into the vehicles. This was our last visit. You should have let us go. Now we'll have to stage a shifta raid on the mission, set a fire and be on our way. You and your friends will find your places in heaven tonight."

"Look, whoever you are," Matt said, "you can't get away with this. Even though you kill us, the police will know you were here. They'll catch you."

"Sorry, nice try. We're in the middle of the desert. Bandits from Somalia and the Sudan come through here all the time and commit murders and robberies. Some of them are pretty sophisticated. In this case they'll destroy the radio and set fire to some buildings before they leave. And, of course, they'll have come after we're gone. We'll tell the commissioner all was in order when we left. Maybe we'll take a couple of you with us and leave you half way to Marsabit. I don't think I'm up to shooting three or four people tonight."

"You can't shoot all of us if we rush you," Matt said.

"I can try. Now be quiet. All four of you get up slowly and walk over to the far wall."

They complied.

"Stand three feet from the wall facing it, put your hands as high as you can and lean against the wall."

They took the position he ordered.

"Now slide your feet away from the wall. Further."

They shuffled away.

"Move at least two meters apart."

After the group had positioned itself along the wall,

Juraj said, "Sister Columba, get the carving knife off the table and cut the cords on the window drapes."

The husky nun did as she was ordered.

"Cut it into one meter pieces."

When she was finished he said, "Tie the hands of your friends behind their backs. I'll test each of them and if they're not tight, you're dead right now."

Sister Columba tied the hands of the three behind their backs.

"Put the knife on the table and move next to Stark while I check the ties. Then I'll take care of you."

Juraj kept his gun on Sister Columba as he walked over to the wall. With the gun in his right hand he pulled with his left at the cords binding the wrists of Brother Sebastian then Sister Brendan. As he did the same to Matt, Matt brought up his right foot up and back and drove his desert boot heel under Juraj's right kneecap.

Juraj screamed with pain and instinctively grabbed at his knee with his free left hand. As the hand holding the gun moved out and away from his body to balance himself, the edge of Sister Columba's right hand struck sharply into the inside of the Juraj's right wrist. The blow to the wrist involuntarily loosened Juraj's grasp on the gun and a slap by Sister Columba's left hand on the back of Juraj's gun hand knocked the weapon to the floor.

Sister Columba, her right hand opened as if holding an apple, but with the fingers stiff and straight, drove her fingers into Juraj eyes. He screamed and grabbed his face.

After the initial kick, Matt turned. He now drove a kick with his left foot toward the blinded Juraj's groin. He missed his target but hit the inner thigh, giving Sister

Columba enough time to pick up the Walther. She pointed it at Juraj.

"Okay, Monsignor, don't do anything fast," she said.

Juraj slowly uncoiled, pain on his face, his eyes watering. Sister repeated her order. Juraj slowly moved himself over to a chair and sat. His head was down and his hands still covered his eyes. Although in pain, his eyesight was recovering. He could see shapes. The ample frame of Sister Columba was outlined six yards in front of him. He made out the shine off the carving knife behind his right foot where it had ended up. Juraj deliberately bent over and picked up the knife.

"Sister, you're not about to shoot anyone. Give me the gun."

"No, drop the knife."

Juraj stood up slowly and took a step toward the nun.

Matt stepped forward toward the man who slashed out at Matt's face. Arms still bound, Matt turned his shoulder toward the knife and took a cut through his shirt and into his left shoulder. He fell back.

"Stop," the nun said sharply.

Juraj turned toward her, the knife in his right hand low by his side, the point forward and slightly raised so it could inflict an upward slashing wound to the stomach. His left arm was extended toward the blurry figure of the nun. An easy target, he thought.

The others had turned and were watching the drama. Matt had fallen to the floor. Sister held the gun in her right hand.

"Give me the gun, Sister," Juraj said in a threatening hiss as he took another step toward her. Sister Columba now held the gun in front of her with both hands. A voice from the past entered Columba's head, "Squeeze the trigger, Lena. Don't jerk it. Squeeze."

Juraj recognized experience in the posture and lunged at the nun. She squeezed the trigger twice.

Both bullets entered Juraj's chest inches apart. Juraj dropped in mid stride. With amazing calm, Sister Columba picked up the knife. With one eye on Juraj she cut the others free. There was no need to watch him, he was bleeding profusely and not moving. Nor would he move again of his own volition.

The two shots had torn up the lung or heart. Columba bent over to examine her victim. "He's dead. Died almost instantly," she said. Then she turned her attention to Matt's wound. "It's not deep. Let's get something to bandage it."

Sister Brendan turned to Sister Columba. "How in the world?"

"Like you, I wasn't always a nun. I'm from Derry. One of my friends was killed by the British on Bloody Sunday. I was an easy recruit for the extreme wing of the IRA. I received some pretty intensive training in my day. It came back too easily."

"That's obvious, and fortunate for us," Matt said as he held a napkin to his cut.

"I learned that you don't stand and talk to someone who wants to kill you. That's only in the movies or books. I lost a close friend that way when a Prods took him out."

"You saved our lives. Thank you," Matt said as normal color slowly returned to his face.

Brother Sebastian was still dazed. "What about the driver?"

"We dismissed the staff after they served us. I don't think they heard anything through these thick walls. Let's check on the driver though," Brendan said. Then she gabbed more napkins to make a bandage until they could get to the clinic.

Brother Sebastian turned out the lights and slid out the door. In a few minutes he was back.

"Juraj's driver killed Daniel. He must have heard something. He and his vehicle are gone. He took at least five of the cases of wire from the basement."

"Let's clean up this mess," Sister Brendan directed. She went to the clinic for dressings to bandage Matt. She cleaned up the blood from Juraj and covered his body. Then she went out to take care of Daniel.

Sister Columba finally realized what she had done and sank into a soft chair. Matt offered her the medicine of choice, a cup of hot tea. She held it in both hands and sipped while the shocked look slowly left her face.

"My God, now we add a dead Monsignor to the gold. What else?" Columba said.

"Hopefully nothing," Matt, feeling more stable, replied.

Everyone sat and looked at each other to avoid looking at the body on the floor.

Finally Matt said, "Let's get out of this room and try to figure out what's happened and what we do next."

Chapter 15

The Decision

They moved into the conference room to be away from the body. Sister Brendan brought fresh tea for the group. As she offered something stronger, Matt pointed out that they had enough stimulation to last for a while. They needed to let the adrenaline settle.

They sat silently around the table. Finally, Brother Sebastian said, "I knew that this was going nowhere good, but I had no way to stop it. Whenever I complained I was told that the money was going to good causes and that it would serve no useful purpose for me to be taken back to Europe and be tried as a war criminal."

"Brother," Sister Brendan said, "there was no chance of that. You were cruelly used and deceived."

"Do we have to tell the authorities anything?" Sister Columba asked.

"Yes, we can't just have people disappearing and have dead bodies lying around." Brendan said. "We have to put an end to this or they, whoever they are, will come again. Not only that, they'll want the gold the driver took and whatever's left. We've got to preserve the mission and our work here. The only way that I can see to do it is to tell the commissioner what happened here and ask for government protection."

"Wait a minute," Matt said. "You've got to go against the Vatican here."

"What's that all about? Do you know Sebastian?" Brendan asked.

"I've thought about that a lot. I don't think there's any official connection. When I went to Rome some of the priests at St. Gerolomo had great sympathy for the Nazis. They helped some escape. But it was on an individual basis. In recent years I'm not sure that the people who came were even clergy. There were little errors in how they handled themselves. Certainly Juraj's conduct was not something that he learned in a seminary. He may not have been a priest."

"He sure wasn't when I met him in Vienna," Matt told them at the meeting. "Don't you know for sure?" Matt asked.

"No," both Sebastian and Brendan replied.

"All right," Sister Brendan continued. "Here's what we're going to do. When we are done here, Matt and Sebastian will have another look around the area to see if everything is quiet. Be careful. Then come back and load the bodies into the Range Rover. Can you use your arm, Matt?"

"Yes."

"Fine. Don't be seen. I don't want to upset the staff. Put a small sample of the gold and supplies in the vehicle for a trip to Marsabit. Sebastian, you'll have to sleep with the vehicle. Sorry. We'll take the pistol and one of the weapons in case we run into the driver on the way to Marsabit. I hope one of you can figure out how to use them because we're going to leave our marksman, Sister Columba, here with the other weapons in case we get any unfriendly visitors. I intend to tell Commissioner Kamala everything and see what he says. Matt, one thing bothers me. Do you or your bosses have any part of this intrigue?"

Matt was surprised. He hesitated. "No, well. . .I don't think so. I know that I have nothing to do with it and I presume that the people who hired me don't. But frankly, I don't know them that well. The only thing that was strange was the meeting in Vienna. "

Matt told them how after the Vienna meeting he was stopped at the airport and questioned by the U.S. and Austrian officials. Monsignor Juraj, if he was a monsignor, seemed to be the connecting link.

Sister Brendan continued. "We'll have breakfast and be on the road at dawn. Add a prayer for a safe journey to your night prayers. Good night."

As Matt was falling to sleep he thought about what would have happened if Juraj had swung higher and gotten his throat or face. Thank God he still had some reaction time and hadn't been drinking.

During breakfast, Moses maneuvered the vehicle out of the compound onto the dusty corrugated road to Marsabit. The road was listed as a Class C primary road on the map and the one hundred and five miles was bumpy and slow.

Averaging about twenty miles an hour, including a short rest stop at Kalacha Dida Spring, it took them until a little after noon to reach the sandy soil, acacia trees and bush that was the welcome mat for the forested mountain that housed Marsabit.

As they pulled into the police compound, they were surprised to see the Rover the driver had taken parked outside the commissioner's headquarters. Because of that sighting, they didn't notice another civilian vehicle in the lot. Heavy traffic for this remote outpost.

"Leave the bodies in the back and hide the guns under the seats. All we need to do is walk in a police station armed to the nines," Sister Brendan said. "Moses, please stay with the vehicle."

They walked in the door and went up to the sharply dressed soldier at the desk. "Good day. I'm Sister Brendan from North Horr. We need to see the commissioner."

"Ah, yes Sister, you are most welcome. The commissioner has been expecting you. Please follow me."

"Expecting us?" The second surprise in a few minutes. Puzzled looks passed among them as they followed the soldier down the hallway to the commissioner's office.

Kamala rose as they entered. "Jambo, Sister. Habari gani. It is not often that we get a visit from you. You are most welcome. Hello, Matt. And you are Brother Sebastian, I believe. Let's have some tea and you can tell me why you are here."

"Well, Commissioner, it's a complicated story," Sister Brendan said, as the group took the chairs opposite Kamala's desk. "We ask your indulgence. I think we should let Brother Sebastian tell you his story first."

"Fine, I find that patience is a great aid to solving most problems. Tell me the story."

Brother Sebastian told the commissioner a shorter version of his history, much as he had told Sister and Matt, including how he came to be in Kenya and how each year he was visited by what he thought were representatives of the Vatican who took off spools of gold.

Sebastian added that on one occasion he was told to deliver a portion of the wire to a certain person at the Vatican Embassy in Nairobi. He was never asked to take it out of the country.

At the end, the commissioner said, "A very intriguing story, Brother. Now I'd like to hear more current history. Someone tell me about recent events. Something that is in my jurisdiction."

Sister Brendan took over the narration. She told about the arrival of Juraj, the confrontation and the shooting. She concluded by telling him that the bodies were in the vehicle outside.

Kamala raised his eyebrows. "Well, it looks like the culprit is not here. Who'd think that mild Sister Columba was a marksman? I'll have to check the Interpol data on her. I trust that she has not fled to Somalia while we are here talking."

Sister Brendan gasped. "I resent that. If she had not acted we would all be dead. She was entirely justified. Someone had to stay at the mission while we came here."

"You may think that she was justified, but we let courts decide that here, as they do in Ireland." Kamala turned to Matt. "What's your part in all this? Things were quiet until you showed up."

"No part in this at all except I was accosted by Juraj like all of us here."

"Well, you're involved now. We need all the particulars about your principals in Houston so we can check them out. In the meantime, you can all be our guests in Nairobi. We also have a presumption of innocence here but we'd like you to be handy. Keep you as material witnesses, so to speak."

"No," Sister Brendan said. "I need to go back to the mission. We need to keep it staffed. This is clearly something out of our control. We and the nomads should not suffer because of the evil done in Europe by who knows who."

"Sister, with all due respect, you're not in charge here," Kamala said firmly. "I have a man in jail whom we found with a supply of gold and now I have two dead men. We'll remove the bodies from your vehicle and place them in a cooler place. We also have unauthorized weapons. I'm sworn to uphold the law. What do you suggest I do? Let a possible murderer and smuggler go free? I'm afraid that you are not in a position to dictate what happens."

Matt interrupted. "I'd like to call my embassy."

"So would I," both Sister Brendan and Brother Sebastian said.

"Wonderful," Kamala said. "We'll have diplomats running around and being unduly officious. One of which, the Vatican representative, might be involved in gold smuggling."

"We're innocent of any wrongdoing. Charging us

will do no one any good," Sister Brendan said, raising her normally soft Irish voice.

Kamala's visage softened. "You maybe right, Sister. But I think that you'll appreciate that you're in an awkward position. What I believe is, as your Texas oilmen might say, you're between a rock and a hard place."

"What's the point of all this badgering," Matt asked, getting irritated at his friend "It's not like you."

"Sorry. I may have overdone it, but I needed to emphasize the seriousness of your position."

"We know that."

"I may have a solution." He paused to let the thought sink in. "It'll require your cooperation, not only now, but in the future. It also may put you in danger but not as much danger as you could be in now."

"You mean you get to keep the gold. Then we promise to keep quiet about it and you let us go," Matt said.

"Ah, Matt," Kamala laughed. "I thought you knew me better than that. You've been reading too many of those American stories about corrupt police and politicians. No, my proposition will help you, the mission and many other people. However, I felt I had to be firm to focus your attention."

Matt was not appeased. "We were focused when we came here. Last night did that. Let's hear your proposal."

"All right, let me get my friend."

Kamala left the room and came back with the man Matt immediately recognized from his interrogation at the Vienna airport. Sean Casey, the US government official who didn't exist.

"Matt, I believe that you know Sean Casey. Mr. Casey, this is Sister Brendan and Brother Sebastian."

Everyone exchanged greetings.

Before Matt could start, Casey said, "Thanks to modern technology and the absence of any eavesdropping laws here, I heard the stories you told the Commissioner. Actually, I knew Brother Sebastian's story. We also had a long conversation with the driver the Commissioner's people picked up last night so, we knew a little about what happened at the mission. We appreciate the additional information."

"Who is we?" Matt asked. "And who the hell are you?"

"Let's just say that I represent an organization whose interests coincide with yours at this time. That's all you need to know. Here's our proposal.

"We'd like Sisters Brendan and Columba and Brother Sebastian to resume their good works at the mission. This would include the safeguarding and distribution of what remains of the gold. In fact we'll return the gold the driver took. In return we'll escort the driver out of the country."

"Oh no," Sister Brendan said. "It's pretty obvious to me that this is gold taken from people in prison camps or stolen from the Church. I want no part of it."

"Hear me out, Sister," Casey said. "You're partly right. Other portions of the gold were stolen from legitimate governments before the end of the war. In 1944, with the help of some Catholic priests, the Nazis transferred large quantities of gold and currency to

Switzerland. Smaller quantities were taken to Rome, as Sebastian has told us, to finance Krizaris forces and to finance the escape routes.

"The activity for which Brother Sebastian was recruited was a little private enterprise. Some in-fighting in the bad guys' camp. God helps those who help themselves," he observed dryly. "The private operation sent the gold you have to Kenya. A small group of non-German SS officers, mainly Croatians and Austrians, felt that the Germans would cut them out from their share so they decided to set up their own little nest egg to supplement what they got from the Germans. That was one reason it worked so well. They didn't need large amounts of money."

"But why keep it going?" Matt asked.

"Because we know it's here, and we want to know where it goes. This is what we call a 'honey pot' operation, and it's quite successful. For years we've traced the gold to people in hiding around the world. That way we were able to keep tabs on people we're interested in, and in some cases have invited them to join us for a visit, or a trial. Most of them have committed atrocities."

"I haven't heard of many being arrested or extradited," Matt said.

"True, but heart attacks and car accidents do not make the international news. Such news, however, does circulate in the right circles."

"But the war was so long ago. Aren't most of the war criminals dead or very old men?"

"To be more accurate very old men and women. Yes, that's true, but the Nazi mentality isn't dead. You've read about the skinheads, terrorists and the like. Extreme rightist parties in Germany and Austria have gotten stronger. Worse, certain of the fascist groups have made connections with terrorist groups and financed them with money such as you have at the mission. The bombing of the US Embassy in Nairobi was financed by someone."

"If you know about them, why not arrest them?"

"If only it were so simple. If we did arrest them, others would spring up. No, we like to do it this way. We follow the money, watch the activity and if things look too serious, take action."

"Once again, who is we? Are you US government?"

"No. Let's just say that my organization has long experience in trying to protect ourselves, and the US government doesn't find our activities inconsistent with their interests."

"That's pretty vague."

"That's how it has to be. Think about it."

"What about my employers in Houston?"

"They're opportunists. We think they got rumors of possible hidden gold in the Chalbi from one of their relatives who had been an American intelligence officer in Italy at the end of World War II. Having a little more than the usual quota of greed and also having more money than brains, they thought that you, through your contacts here, could get them a seismic contract.

"With that in hand they could send people and equipment to the desert to do a real search without arousing too much suspicion. I don't think they knew it was in the mission and I don't think that they knew that if they took the gold they would stand a pretty good chance of being killed by its keepers. In any event, the Kenyan government is going to turn down your request for a contract. It will announce that the Kenyan National Oil Company will do its own seismic program next year with money obtained from the International Monetary Fund."

"What about the other bodies that have been found?" Matt asked.

"Some were really killed by bandits. A couple of the others we suspect were killed by Juraj's group who trailed them up here like they trailed you. We really don't know," the commissioner answered.

"So what about us?" Brother Sebastian asked.

"If you just resume your prior activities at the mission, you'll be okay. The official story is that Monsignor Juraj and his driver were killed by shiftas. Bodies, partly decomposed and torn by scavengers were found by Kenyan authorities."

"I think this is what is referred to as a win-win situation in some circles," Kamala observed.

"I don't think we have a choice-choice," Matt said.

Kamala smiled. "Well, your sense of humor is making a feeble come back."

"There is no question that I'd like to go back and resume my work at the mission," Sister Brendan said. "Especially in view of the alternatives. I presume we can tell Sister Columba about all this."

"Ah, the gunman, yes, but no one else."

"I, too, would like to go back to the mission," Brother Sebastian said.

"Good, thy will be done. We thought that you might make this decision so we had your vehicle refueled and fresh water put in your jerricans. Stay the night at the lodge if you like."

Matt and the two religious agreed. Casey declined the offer, saying he wanted to start back immediately. The commissioner offered to send one of his vehicles with him as far as Isiolo.

"Let me thank you for your continued cooperation, Commissioner." Casey shook hands with Stark, Sister Brendan and Brother Sebastian. "We've done a just thing. I think the God we all worship will be pleased. Shalom," he said as he left them.

The commissioner also offered a driver to take Matt and Moses back to Nairobi. The next morning the commissioner came to the lodge at dawn to say good-bye.

Matt walked out to the Land Rover with them. "To say the least, it's been an experience, one I can't tell anyone about except to say I met some unforgettable people. I wish you well," he said to Sister Brendan and Brother Sebastian.

"Thanks, Matt. God speed you home. Watch your shoulder. We cleaned it pretty good and you should have no trouble. Enjoy your family and be more cautious about your next consulting job," Sister Brendan said.

Matt laughed. "I think this is the last one."

Sebastian and Brendan got into the vehicle and started down the road that would take them through the forest and out into the desert. Matt waved until they were out of sight. Then he got in the police vehicle for the return to Nairobi and his old life.

Once in the Rover he turned to Moses and said, "Casey said something about releasing a story that the

Monsignor and his driver were killed by bandits. I thought the driver was still alive."

Moses shrugged. "I don't know."

On the two-day drive he concluded that at least one part of his quest might be successful. At the overnight stop at the Mount Kenya Safari Club he phoned Melanie.

"Melanie, Matt Stark here. I'll be back in Nairobi tomorrow. I'd like to take you to the Horseman Restaurant for dinner. After her reply he said. "Please reconsider. I think I have a handle on that problem. A little sobering experience to use a phrase." He paused a moment for her answer.

"Great. Thanks for a second chance. The trip? Well it was interesting. Hurt my shoulder when I fell out of the Rover but other than that uneventful." Matt rolled his eyes. "I didn't find anything to encourage looking for oil but I met some unique individuals. You haven't resigned or anything? No. Good. Let's talk about your plans and mine."

Epilogue

Matt Stark returned to Texas. He reported to Billy Bob and Big Tex that the Kenyan government would make no deal and would handle further exploration themselves. He collected his pay and expenses. On his return to Austin he sold the house at the lake where he had lived with Carol and moved into a condominium in the city to enjoy life in a multi-generational, multi-cultural environment. He did volunteer work and visited his children and grandchildren with regularity. He and **Melanie** were in contact frequently by e-mail and phone. He met her in the spring in Washington, D.C. She resigned from the State department and was working as a consultant in D.C.

Sisters Brendan and Columba stayed at the mission for five and seven years respectively, at which times they were permanently rotated back to Ireland. Sister Brendan lives in the Republic. Sister Columba lives in the north in Balleycastle. Any involvement in IRA activity had been expunged from her record.

Commissioner Kamala worked until the Kenyan

retirement age of fifty-five. He then moved back to his shamba in the west of Kenya where he lived peacefully with his wife. They periodically made trips to England to visit their children and grandchildren. The trips were paid for from monthly payments made to his account in a bank in the Jersey Islands from a bank in Liechtenstein.

The bodies of **Monsignor Juraj** and his driver were found in the Chalbi desert. They had been ravaged by scavengers but were still identifiable. The police report concluded that they had probably been robbed and killed by bandits, most likely poachers from Somalia. The Monsignor's body was buried at a funeral Mass in Nairobi after some confusion over his identity with religious authorities in Rome. The driver had no known relatives and was buried at the Mission.

Brother Sebastian died a few years later at age 79, having never returned to Italy. He was cremated and his ashes buried at the Mission in North Horr. In a symbolic gesture, Sister Brendan put on his funeral pyre the last spool of "electric wire" that Brother Sebastian had brought with him when he first came to Kenya and which he had watched over in performing his duties as supply officer for the mission. He was not replaced by the Order as none of his fellow religious wished to go to the desert. Not even for forty days.

Dinko Sakic was the Deputy Commander of the Jasenovac camp under Croatia's wartime government and the commander the Stara Gradiska concentration camp during WW II. In June 1998, at seventy-six, he was extradited from Argentina to Croatia to stand trial for war crimes connected with operations of the camps. According to the July 26, 1998 edition of the "New York Times," his wife, **Esperanza Sakic**, was also extradited for alleged illegal activities while she served as a camp guard at Stara Gradiska between 1942 and 1945.

On August 22nd, 1999 the Kenyan government announced the closing of the border with Somalia following an attack by four hundred Somali militiamen on a Kenyan Army patrol. Somalia has lacked a central government since 1991.

About the Author

Jack Rosshirt is a retired attorney who spent over twenty years in the international petroleum business, with emphasis on Africa and the Middle East. He has lived in Tehran, Iran, Nairobi, Kenya, and Copenhagen. Prior to that he served in the US Army Counter-Intellingence Corps. He is a graduate of the University of Notre Dame and its Law School.

He uses his insights into a variety of political, economic, cultural and social philosophies gained through his travels and negotiations with international businesses and foreign governments to add background and flavor to his writings.

Jack and his wife of 45 years have raised five sons and are the grandparents of seven grandsons and one granddaughter.

In addition to writing, Jack has handled pro bono litigation and mediation. He is an avid tennis fan and a certified tennis official.

To order additional copies of
Kenyan Quest

Name _____

Address _____

_____

$14.95 x _____ copies =   _____

State Sales Tax
(Texas residents add 8.25% sales tax)   _____

Please add $3.50 postage and
handling per book   _____

Total amount due: _____

Please send check or money order for books to:

Jack Rosshirt
P.O. Box 5276
Austin, TX 78763

For a complete catalog of our books, visit our site at
http://www.WordWright.biz

Printed in the United States
1019800001B/4-27